DREAM CHASER

**Hodder
Children's
Books**

a division of Hodder Headline Limited

Also by Joan O'Neill

Daisy Chain War
Bread and Sugar
Daisy Chain Dream
Daisy Chain Days

Fallen Star

Acknowledgements

My heartfelt thanks to the following:

The Ellis Island Foundation – the most diligent of family history detectives – for their invaluable help when I visited there last year, and to the members of my family who travelled with me on my quest to trace the journeys of my immigrant ancestors, and were such good company and fun.

The members of my Writer's Group: Sheila Barrett, Julie Parsons, Catherine Phil MacCarthy, Cecilia McGovern, Renate Ahrens-Kramer, and Cathy Leonard, for their excellent advice, and criticism.

The staff at Deansgrange Library and Ballywaltrim Library for help with research – nothing was too much trouble.

My art teacher, Olivia Hayes, for her excellent tuition, and all my artist friends who provided essential relaxation and companionship throughout.

Mary Byrne for taking such good care of me on my publicity tour.

My editor, Emily Thomas, for her expert guidance, encouragement, and belief in my work.

Jonathan Lloyd and Camilla Goslett for all their work on my behalf, and for having my best interests at heart.

All of my family and friends for the love and kindness they showered on me, particularly my daughters Elizabeth and Laura for their excellent advice, encouragement, and constructive criticism at all stages of this story. And my Son, Robert, for 'technical management'.

This book is dedicated to the members of my family, and the generations of Irish women who emigrated to America and whose important contribution to its economy and development deserves a celebrated place in history.

Copyright © 2006 Joan O'Neill

First published in Great Britain in 2006 by Hodder Children's Books

The right of Joan O'Neill to be identified as the Author
of the Work has been asserted by her in accordance with the
Copyright, Designs and Patents Act 1988.

1

A Catalogue record for this book is available from the British Library

ISBN 0 340 91148 4

Typeset in Bembo by Avon DataSet Ltd,
Bidford on Avon, Warwickshire

Printed and bound in Great Britain by Bookmarque Ltd, Croydon, Surrey

The paper and board used in this paperback by Hodder Children's Books are
natural recyclable products made from wood grown in sustainable forests. The
manufacturing processes conform to the environmental regulations of the
country of origin.

Hodder Children's Books
a division of Hodder Headline Ltd
338 Euston Road
London NW1 3BH

'Take off your hat,' the King said to the Hatter.

'It isn't mine,' said the Hatter.

'*Stolen!*' the King exclaimed, turning to the jury, who instantly made a memorandum of the fact.

'I keep them to sell,' the Hatter added as an explanation: 'I've none of my own. I'm a hatter.'

From *Alice in Wonderland* – Lewis Carroll

One

It was a hot afternoon in the summer of 1923. A motionless day with a satiny-blue sky and amber-coloured trees steeped in sunlight. White butterflies flitted between the low boughs of the laden apple trees. Gnats hung in the air. Seduced by hot sun, the chirping birds, and the sweet, ripe smell of apples, I abandoned the fruit bushes I was stripping and lay down on a shady patch of grass soaking up the beauty all around me, wanting the calm of this perfect day to go on for ever, knowing that it wouldn't. Already the leaves from the trees were beginning to fall, and I could smell autumn in the air.

The limpid stillness was broken by the shrieks and cries of 'Got you'. Shep, our sheep dog, barked madly as he raced around with Alice and Lucy, my sisters, who were chasing one another, darting among the bushes, stopping only to cram handfuls of luscious berries into their mouths before continuing their frantic game.

I was fourteen years old. Alice, at thirteen, was next to

me in age. A tall, slender girl with a mass of rich-brown curls, she was as bright as a firecracker, and agile as a cat. Noisy and fun-loving, she thrived on adventure. We argued a lot but made up quickly. We giggled about the local boys, and told each other secrets long into the night in our shared bed. Lucy, who was ten, was a fragile ten-year-old waif, with thick plaits like ropes, and saucer-blue eyes. She hung around Mam all the time so we called her 'Mam's apron strings'.

Tired of their game they both flung themselves down beside me, flat on their stomachs, their long thin legs in the air.

'Johnny Sheerin's back home,' Alice said, squinting up at me through her glow of tangled hair.

'No!' I was surprised because Johnny had left home six months ago to work in the construction business in Dublin.

'I met him in the shop. He's back to help his dad out with the harvest. Then he'll be off again. That's what he said.'

'Johnny's lucky, I'd love to get away from here,' I sighed, looking longingly towards the sea.

'Why?' Lucy asked, a puzzled look in her eyes.

'I want to see the world,' I said. 'And besides, there's not much for me here.'

'There's us,' Lucy pointed out.

'What I mean is that nothing ever happens here. This place is as dull as ditch water.'

'There's not much fun to be had,' Alice agreed.

Lucy grimaced. 'There's our dancing classes, and there's the Harvest Festival,' she offered, as an example of excitement.

'You think that's fun?' Alice snorted.

The village revolved around the Harvest Festival. There was always a brass band and processions, tea and stale buns in the local hall, and an Irish dancing competition afterwards. There was nothing exciting about that unless you won a medal or a cup.

Irked, Lucy bit her lip. 'I love it here, I *never* want to leave.' Shadows danced across her face as she lifted it to follow the flight of a gull into the cloudless sky.

I gazed past our blazing fields to the sapphire-blue sea, still as a sleeping tiger, filigrees of sunlight darting through it like flashing diamonds, its small white-capped waves washing rhythmic to shore. It was hard to believe that this was the same treacherous sea that damned our town to bad weather each winter, and threatened our lives. Our village had lived at the mercy of the storms for centuries – whirlwinds of rain and crashing thunder did untold damage to our crops, and scared us to death.

'If you do leave here, Ellie, where will you go?' An anxious Lucy was biting her lip with her new frilly-edged teeth.

'America,' I said resolutely, gazing out towards the North Atlantic. 'Aunt Mabel says it's an exciting place where you don't know what's going to happen next.'

'I'll come with you,' Alice said, excitedly jumping to her feet, ready for off that very minute.

Alarmed, Lucy said, 'But what'll I do if you both go? Who will I have to play with?'

I tickled her arm with a blade of grass. 'Don't fret, it's not going to happen. Dad wouldn't hear of letting me go while Ed's away. I'm needed to help out on the farm. Now, let's finish picking these bushes, Mam's waiting on us.' I reached for Lucy's hand to coax her up. 'Come on, lazybones, we're nearly done.'

Grimacing, she got to her feet.

When we'd filled the white enamel pan with the squashed fruit, I left my sisters pinching and mock-punching one another and carried the pan down the slope to the scullery.

The kitchen was filled with the smell of cooking fruit. Mam was standing at the stove vigorously stirring the big aluminium pot. Her neck was red as the jam that bubbled and splashed on to the sides.

She slapped a sliver on to a saucer, and tipped it sideways. Rainbows of light shot through it as it wrinkled like the sea in the wind. 'Set,' she declared, casting her expert eye over it. 'There.' She straightened herself. 'Now I can get the next lot started.' Sunlight from the window shone on her tired face as she lifted the heavy pot and took it to the sink to cool. Watching her lumbering about in her loose overall, my heart flipped over.

'Sit down and have a cup of tea first, Mam. The midwife says you're to take it easy.'

As she sipped her tea slowly, the tension eased from Mam's face. I lined up the glossy, scalded jars and busily crammed each one full of the luscious dark fruit, then labelled each jar 'Blackberry 1923' and placed them on a shelf alongside the rest of the jams. There were preserves and home-made bottled wine on the scullery shelves, each season depicted on the label of its jar.

Spring was trapped in the clarity of the elderflower wine, summer in the strawberry, plum, and loganberry jams. The crab-apple jelly shone the dull rose of autumn, and winter was in the burnished gold of the marmalade.

Jam was one of Mam's money-making schemes. The surplus was sold to the village shop along with the eggs, and she spent the profits on shoes and schoolbooks for us.

The scullery door banged and Dad came into the kitchen.

'Smells good,' he said, tilting back the peak of his cap, and sitting down to remove his heavy boots. 'I suppose it's bread and jam for tea,' he teased her.

'Won't do you any harm for once,' she said, her bright blue eyes crinkling at the corners as she smiled at him.

'We'll start saving the hay tomorrow. I'll want all hands on deck,' he said, going to the sink, washing his hands. 'We're lucky with this year's crop. It's dried out nicely.'

'But I promised Mabel that Ellie would help her with her big wedding order,' Mam said.

'Mabel will just have to manage without her. The haymaking won't wait,' Dad said brusquely.

'Can't you let her off for one day, Matt?' Mam pleaded.

'Please Dad,' I begged, resenting his dependence on me.

'Only if Alice is willing to do your stint.'

'I am,' Alice said, coming into the kitchen.

'Just the one day, mind,' Dad warned.

'Can I help too?' Lucy asked, trailing in behind Alice.

'No, you stay and keep your mother company.'

'Please, Dad,' she begged.

'No.' His jaw was set firmly and a deep line furrowed his brow, a sign that there was no point in arguing any further with him.

Dad was a strong, handsome man, with sharp blue eyes, a weather-beaten face, and hair the colour of straw from the sun and wind. He was a farmer-fisherman. As soon as the hay was saved and things were slack on the farm he would fish with the local fishermen for the rest of the winter.

After an early summons from Brendan Sheerin, our nearest neighbour, he would go out in the misty dawn, and return at dusk. Sometimes, he wouldn't return until well into the night. In stormy weather, Alice and I would lie in bed listening to the rain beating against the window panes and the wind slapping against the walls of our cottage, scared stiff, imagining his boat being sucked down into the merciless sea. But Dad was a great fisherman. He could gauge the moods of the sea, and he'd always come home.

Come springtime, he'd be back on the farm to plant the crops and we would all be much happier.

Mam was fond of telling us the story of how my Dad, Matthew O'Rourke, had spotted her, Patricia Casey, in the town one market day, and had fallen head over heels in love with her. Fifteen years older than Mam, and with a small farm and cottage by the sea in Lisheen 'a village ten minutes outside Cork city' he'd inherited from his bachelor uncle, he was ready to settle down. She often used to say that he had plagued her until she agreed to marry him, though we knew by the tone of her voice that she'd been smitten by him too. Carefree, romantic, a dreamer, she was completely different to Dad in every way. Though cautious around him, because he was in charge, she loved him deeply.

I left our village school that summer. It had provided me with a basic education. The long, narrow building was divided into two classrooms: juniors and seniors. Mrs Crotty, our teacher, a sour-faced, frightening figure with wire glasses and hair coiled in earphones, taught us as far as second class. She'd crammed us with sums and writing, and had whacked us with her ruler if she caught us off-guard, smirking or nudging one another.

Miss Smith, who taught seniors, was young and gentle. In her sweet voice she had taught us to sing and recite poetry, and had encouraged us to write stories. Hunched into long, narrow desks, we'd learned all about the great wars and could rattle off the dates of important battles. We'd studied the world's geography from enormous maps pinned to the wall. When she'd explained that we were now living in our new free state, and said that she didn't feel too confident about it, I was more curious than the rest of the class and asked her questions. Far from losing patience with me, Miss Smith found my curiosity endearing, though she wasn't sure of the answers.

On the last day of school I lingered on, stacking the books away in the cupboard, reluctant to leave the deserted classroom. Sadly, I looked for the last time at the long narrow scored desks, the empty inkwell, the cast-iron stove in the corner that we relied on for heat in the cold winters, and the old map on the wall, and felt desolate. I wanted to stay on in this cocoon of learning, with its smoky atmosphere and soot-stained walls, but I had learned everything Miss Smith had to teach me.

Outside, Miss Smith caught up with me. 'Have you persuaded your dad to let you go to the secondary school, Ellie?'

'Not yet,' I said uneasily.

'You're a clever girl, it would be a shame not to continue with your education.'

Full of brilliant fantasies about going off to the Mercy Convent boarding school in Cork city, where my Aunt Mary was a nun, I'd walked home dreaming about a world beyond my imagination.

I told Dad what Miss Smith had said, but he wouldn't hear of it. 'You're needed here to help out,' he said. It was true. Since my brother Ed had joined the Irregulars (a group of men who were against this new free state) earlier in the year, and had gone off to a training camp at a secret location, and Mam was expecting another baby, they were depending on me to do all the chores around the house. I'd soak the sheets in the big tub in the yard, then sneak off to the lower field to read one of the wonderful books Miss Kenny, the librarian, picked out for me, and through it's pages escaped to another world, for a short time at least.

Two

Aunt Mabel was a milliner. She had trained in New York with Jeffrey Rowe, a famous hat designer, and had lived there for years. She had a fine shop styled on the one that she had managed in New York. Gilt mirrors lined the walls and showed off the beautiful hats on shelves and on stands from all angles. The counter was piled with soft berets. At the rear of the shop there was a tiny sitting room where she served tea to her customers, who reclined on a pink velvet couch scattered with soft satin cushions. It was a warm, comfortable room, a social meeting place.

The workroom at the back of the shop had a cutting-out table between the two big windows. Shelves full of materials and patterns ran the length of one wall, and there was a table with a gramophone and piles of popular records beside it that Aunt Mabel had brought back with her from New York.

Practical and energetic, she ran her business entirely on her own. Her reputation was so good that she had all the local well-heeled ladies coming to her. Her most fashionable hat style at that time was the cloche: a soft close-fitting helmet-like hat with a small brim. She made her daytime cloches from felt, and set them off with a plain ribbon. Evening cloches were made from velvet or satin, and were embellished with beading, appliqué, or embroidery.

Mabel started me off with the sewing when I was six years old, making dresses and hats for my dolls. As I grew older she taught me how to crochet hats for special occasions like weddings. She let me help her to make trimmings and frames. I learned to block a crown and drape a turban in exquisite material using small stitches. When she had a wedding on, I was allowed to stay with her to help her stitch feathers and costume brooches on bandeaux for bridesmaids, or festoon the wide droopy brims of her beautiful bridal confections with ribbons, artificial flowers, or pheasant and duck feathers collected on our farm. Once she chose a medieval theme for a special occasion and we worked into the night coming up with the most outlandish and wonderful hats, putting on roses so they looked as if they grew there.

Aunt Mabel was very beautiful. When she wore one of her snow-white blouses she looked dazzling. Often she played her long-player when we'd finished work, Mabel dancing around in her Mary-Janes. She'd grab my hand and pull me on to the floor and we'd dance to 'Look For A Silver Lining' from her favourite musical,

Sally, until we were breathless. I learned from her most of the fancy, intricate steps of the quickstep and the tango, before she started me on the Charleston.

In her slack times she renovated her cast-off silk frocks for Mam, Alice and me. I helped her to straighten bodices by letting out seams and gussets, drop waistlines, raise hemlines, adding swags or sailor collars or bits of fur to fancy them up. Occasionally we'd argue over a certain style as we measured and snipped, but I always agreed with her in the end because she was so clever.

Aunt Mabel's elegant manner and her strain of fantasy made her different from everyone else I knew, especially when she reminisced about her days in America while I stitched feathers. Perched on her high stool, sipping her coffee, her cheeks glowing, she recalled her time there. Through her memories I caught a glimpse of shimmering balls, chandeliers, handsome men in naval uniform, and girls in long white frocks all feathered and flounced. There was always a slight twang in her voice as she took me to those magic times. 'The Yanks have standards of living we could never hope to attain. They eat dinner in the evening, and there's wine with each course,' she'd tell me.

The drudgery of the farm was soon forgotten while she talked. I was in another world, half-witless with wonder. I'd beg for more tales saying, 'Oh Aunt Mabel, please tell me more,' and she obliged. She knew that I couldn't get enough of her stories. 'Why did you come back here, Aunt Mabel?' I asked her boldly, after one of her fascinating accounts.

With a far-off look in her eye she told me of her betrothal to a naval officer, an ambitious and charming young man, she said, full of bright hopes and ideas for their future. Soon after their engagement, he'd set sail in his ship for South America and she'd returned home to care for my ailing grandmother. 'I waited for him to send for me when he got back. I'm still waiting,' she added with a little laugh.

'That is so sad!'

'Oh, I'm not unhappy now. I can see that it might not have worked out – and I've got my business. Chandler might have wanted to run it his way, and that would never have suited me. You've always got to be in charge of your own business, Ellie,' she said. 'Once you let anyone else take over, you might as well forget it. You keep that in mind.'

After we finished work we had supper in the warm kitchen, made by Peggy, the servant girl, who had an insatiable curiosity about the people in the town and loved spreading gossip.

That day, Aunt Mabel looked particularly lovely in her black frock with its dropped gold band, a matching gold bandeaux around her bobbed hair. With one of her big, indulgent smiles, she asked me to come through to her bright workroom and poured me coffee from her

14

percolator, another one of her American souvenirs. A smile dimpled her glowing cheeks. 'We're going out for a treat today,' she said, handing me a tiny cupful.

'Where?' I asked excitedly, trying to like the taste of the dark, bitter brew.

'To town for some new material for Lady Mary Grimes's daughter. Hers is going to be the wedding of the year and Lady M wants something different.' Excitedly, she added, 'Would you believe, she sent her butler with the money in advance.'

Before we left, Aunt Mabel decked me out in her smarter clothes. Together we went into town in her pony and trap.

In her close-fitting cloche hat, pulled down over one eye, her neck arched, she paraded around Lennon's draper shop examining the stock with the affected air of a duchess. In the fabric section she took a length of stiff straw that caught her eye and twisted it into the shape of a birdcage. 'What do you think?' she asked, plonking it on my head and, standing me in front of the bevelled mirror, using me as a guinea pig.

'Wonderful!' I said, laughing as I turned it this way and that.

'Wait!' She ransacked a drawer of accessories for a stuffed bird and perched it on the top.

'Marvellous!' I exclaimed.

'I'll take it,' she said to Mrs Lennon, and proceeded to purchase yards of satin, tulle and taffeta in all the latest blues, greens and burgundy colours, and lace and netting for the trimmings. She also bought books on the latest fashions. Mrs Lennon was full of admiration for her handiwork while wrapping up everything. Then I was treated to tea in Foyle's hotel, where our talk was of hats, over dainty cucumber sandwiches and cream cakes. Sipping a gin cocktail, Aunt Mabel looked at me thoughtfully and said, 'Not happy about leaving school, Ellie?'

'Not happy at all,' I said, with a sinking heart. 'I was hoping to go on to the Mercy Convent in Cork. But Dad is dead against it.'

'Do you want me to talk to him?'

'Oh no!' That was the last thing I wanted. He was exasperated with Aunt Mabel's sense of fantasy, and had complained to Mam that her tales of life in America had given me notions beyond my station in life. It was becoming common knowledge in our family that I wanted to follow in Mabel's footsteps and become a bonafide milliner myself.

Aunt Mabel had her own opinion of Dad too, and it was a poor one. She had never understood why Mam had fallen for him. 'Out fishing all day while you're slaving away,' she'd say to Mam when she'd see her tired from all her hard work. Mam would remind her gently that Dad was a fisherman by trade, and that she'd married him for love.

'If you want to run a business you need a proper

education.' Aunt Mabel told me. 'You'll have to go to America to make something of yourself, the way I did.'

'Dad'll never allow it,' I said sadly.

'You don't belong to this remote place, Ellie,' she continued. 'A better world lies ahead for you.' Easier said than done, I thought – but didn't say.

Before we left she took her gold-tooled compact out of her pigskin handbag and applied her lipstick lavishly, then powdered her nose with her large puff in sight of the whole restaurant.

Back in her workroom we worked neatly and briskly on her wide variety of styles, Aunt Mabel humming 'Tee-Oodle-Um-Bum-Bo' to the Jerome Kem jazz tune. In my element, I covered the bride's headband in white satin, sewed clusters of seed pearls on to it, and attached long white ribbons on to either side.

That night, as I lay in the soft bed in the spare room, Aunt Mabel's words of advice rang in my ears – and I made a decision there and then that some day America would be my destiny.

Next morning, Peggy couldn't contain her excitement. 'I hear the railway bridge has been blown up. There'll be no trains for a while!'

'No!' Aunt Mabel's hands fluttered to her face. 'Do the police know who did it?'

'Not yet, but I'm sure they won't be long finding

out, and God help whoever it is when they do.'

Aunt Mabel glanced in my direction. A shiver ran down my spine and I wished I knew where Ed was at that moment.

On the last day of our summer holidays, I went with Alice to help with the haymaking. In the scorched fields, Dad and some neighbours had been hard at work since early morning. I found Alice and some other helpers in the upper field forking the grass, flinging the sweet-smelling swathes up to Paddy-The-Stacker. He was perched on top of the haystack, shaping it. The air hummed with the clang of pitchforks.

'Ellie!' I turned to see Johnny Sheerin standing behind me.

'Hello Johnny.'

Wiping the perspiration from his brow, he threw down his fork and came over to where I stood rooted to the spot. In the year since I'd last seen him he'd changed beyond all recognition. He was taller and his chest was rounded like a barrel. His broad shoulders and forearms rippled with muscles as he lifted his fork to bail the hay. Even though we'd been neighbours all of our lives, I was in awe of him, mainly because of the assurance his good looks gave him that the other boys of my acquaintance didn't have.

'You back for good this time or are you going back up to Dublin?' I asked.

He shook his head, smiling. 'I haven't made up my mind yet. It depends on a lot of things.'

Johnny Sheerin was a hard-working young man. Brendan Sheerin's youngest son, the only one of his three sons who hadn't gone to America. He and my brother Ed were close friends. Both eighteen years old, they were in the same class at school.

'You're not going to ruffle that pretty frock with the haymaking, are you?' he asked with a twinkle of his blue mischievous eyes.

'It's only a frock,' I said, thinking how good it was to see him again.

'Well, you're working with the best pitchers in the county today,' he said, slapping his chest. 'It's a good crop, despite the drought.'

'Rain was prayed for at Mass on Sunday,' I said.

'So I heard,' he said.

'Not by us though. We've prayed for the drought to continue so we can go swimming,' I smiled.

His eyes were the colour of the cloudless sky as he looked at it. 'I'm not sure now if that's a good idea. It's too hot.'

Tearing my eyes from him I took a pitchfork and turned to my task, flinging myself into a flush of activity just to let him see that I was as good as anyone else at the job. The smell of the cut hay was sweetly stifling but I worked on, stoically forking hay up to Paddy, who raked it in to make the butt of the stack.

When the stack was completed, Johnny threw down his pitchfork. 'Thirsty work,' he said, walking over to the back of his hay-cart and pulling a bottle out of a sack. He unwrapped it, removed the cork, and held it out to me. 'Like a swig?' he asked, stretching himself to his magnificent height.

'I'm all right,' I said in a parched voice, too shy to drink in front of him.

'Go on, I know you're dying of thirst,' he coaxed.

I tossed down my fork and succumbed, taking the bottle from him and gulping from it. Suddenly, my stomach felt on fire. Gasping, my cheeks burning, I clumsily handed the bottle back to him. 'I never tasted water like that before. What is it?' I spluttered, my throat crackling like a flame.

'Only a drop of the creatur' for energy you know,' he laughed, and tipped it to his lips.

'Shame on you, giving me drink like that. Dad'll kill you if he finds out.'

'Sure I don't touch a drop, only during the harvest,' he said with a wide smile. In his perfect profile, his glinting, cat-like eyes and curving mouth, I saw temptations more threatening than anything I had yet dreamed of.

'You're as bad as you ever were, Johnny Sheerin,' I said and went back to work.

At noon, Alice and I ate our soda bread and drank our bottles of milk sitting under the shade of a tree. As we finished she said with a sigh, 'Johnny's not bad looking these days, is he?'

'He's all right,' I said with a shrug.

Puzzled, she looked at me. 'I thought you liked him?'

'Time to get back to work,' I said quickly, wrapping up my things and sauntering back to help Paddy start another haystack.

Towards evening, Johnny said, 'Come on, time we had a break, Ellie.'

He lifted me up on to the cart and jumped up beside me. Close up, I could smell his salty skin.

'So, you're working on the farm?'

'Yes. Not by choice; I want to continue with my schooling.'

He leaned towards me, his eyes glittering with merriment. 'How much more education do you need for milking cows and making butter?' he teased.

Furious, I lifted my shoulders defiantly. 'I want to get away from all that.'

'What's stopping you?'

I swallowed the lump in my throat. 'Ed's not around to help out, so I've got to do it.'

He nodded. I suspected that Johnny knew more about Ed's whereabouts than I did, but I didn't dare ask him. I knew that Ed was a member of a group of Irregulars, and that he carried a gun in his pocket, because I often saw him polish it in the barn before disappearing out into the night. I was angry with Ed for deserting us, but this was a family matter, so I changed the subject.

'America is where I'm heading for next,' I said. 'It's a great place. Anything you want to do over there, you can do it, if you believe in yourself. That's what Aunt Mabel says.'

'So I've heard,' Johnny agreed.

There was silence between us, just the sound of the haymaking going on behind us. In the distance, boys dived from the rocks into the sea in an explosion of arms and legs. Johnny said, as unselfconsciously as when we were children, 'I wish we were in the sea with them.'

'So do I,' I said, longingly. We sat silently watching the edge of the sun as it began its slow descent towards the horizon. It was a perfect day. There was magic all around. It was in the sunlit fields and rosy haystacks, in the swaying trees and the sky, blue as a china bowl.

Suddenly, out of nowhere, trench-coated men appeared at the top of the field, guns slung over their shoulders, and walked towards the edge of the wood where they started shooting at trees. The fields resounded with the sound of the shots. Startled, I jumped down from the cart in terror. 'What's happening?'

Johnny gave a flicker of a smile as he jumped down too. 'It's target practice. There's more trouble brewing around these parts.'

I knew that by the sound of their volleys echoing across the valley.

'There'll be hell to pay yet,' he said.

Glancing at him, I longed to bring out into the open the whole question of his and Ed's relationship with the Irregulars, but an instinct prevented me. Dad had forbidden any sort of discussion about the continuing 'disturbances', as he called it.

'Dad has made us all promise to keep out of politics.'

'Why?' His hooded eyes lifted at the corners.

Dad never considered the Irregulars a real, proper army, and thought that they were 'acting the fool' – though I didn't say this to Johnny.

Johnny gave me a sidelong glance. 'You mightn't be able to keep out of it for much longer. Not when you're surrounded by it.'

I shrugged, feigning indifference, realising that Dad's protective instinct towards us could be a drawback.

'Ellie!' Alice was coming towards us. 'I was looking for you. Johnny Sheerin, you're a bad influence on my sister,' she teased him. Alice had always accepted Johnny as someone not to be given any special attention. I envied her this attitude.

He laughed. 'Still as bossy as ever, Alice O'Rourke,' he chided her.

'Are you coming?' she asked me.

'In a minute,' I said, a little impatiently.

'Ellie! Alice!' Dad's voice rang out in the clear air.

'I'd better go,' I said to Johnny. I brushed the hayseeds off my frock and added, 'See you soon' as casually as I could, and scrambled off down the bank after the others, my feet hardly touching the ground.

'There's a dance at the crossroads on Sunday evening. Will you be there?' Johnny called after me.

'I might,' I said, blushing furiously.

'I'll look out for you,' he said.

We were heading home, our shadows flitting ahead of us, when Alice said, 'Well, Johnny Sheerin likes you, Ellie, even if you don't like him . . .'

I kept my eyes on the road so she wouldn't see my burning cheeks.

'But you like him, don't you?'

'We looked at one another and laughed. 'I suppose so,' I said. 'But don't go telling anyone,' I warned, knowing how tactless she could be.

She burst out laughing. ''Course I won't tell.' She leaned forward and whispered. 'He's dead nuts on you, though, Ellie, that's for sure?'

'No, he isn't,' I said, my face turning crimson. But I swept home along the dusty road bursting with happiness.

Three

After the Harvest Festival, the men returned to their fishing. Dad was home late most nights. One night in October, a persistent knocking on the back door and Shep barking woke me. I heard Mam's footsteps in the passage, then the slide back of the bolt of the door, and the sound of low voices in our yard. Suddenly, not a minute later, a loud wail wrenched the air. I leaped out of bed, grabbed my shawl, and ran down the passage, to see Brendan and Johnny Sheerin walking Mam back into the kitchen.

'What's happened? Is it Dad?' I gasped, looking from one of the men to the other.

Johnny Sheerin nodded.

'Where is he?' I asked, my eyes frantically searching their faces.

'He was fishing over by the rocks,' said Brendan. 'When he didn't come back, we went looking for him. We found his boat drifting near Rocky Island but there was no sign of him. We searched everywhere.'

'Are you sure, but are you sure?' Mam burst out, her

chest heaving. Her whole body shook as she resumed her heart-rending cries, like the cries of a wounded animal.

'Get her a drink of water,' Brendan ordered me.

I ran to the yard pump, filled a mug, and held it to her deadly-cold hand. She grasped it and took a sip, looking at Brendan. Suddenly, Shep started barking crazily in the yard.

'Matt!' Mam called out, getting to her feet and hurrying to the door. I made to follow her but Johnny was beside me, his fingers pressing into my flesh as he pulled me to one side.

'He's drowned, isn't he?' No sooner had I said the words than I burst into tears.

'We don't know. The sea was calm, there wasn't even much of a wind. That's the mystery.' He shook his head. 'We'll resume the search at daylight. I'm sure we'll find him.'

'I'm coming down to the beach with you,' I said.

'Me too,' Alice said from the doorway. There was a stubborn look in her eyes as she said, 'I want to be there when you find him.'

Lucy came into the kitchen half-asleep, but when she saw Mam and the state she was in she ran and put her arms around her. Brendan coaxed them both to the settle. He seemed at a loss as to know what to say. Meantime, Johnny stoked up the range and filled the kettle.

'Let's get dressed,' I said, leading Lucy back down the passage.

It was still dark when, tight with dread, we ran down to the beach, fear hurrying us along. The sea was flat, calm as a millpond. All the boats were moored in the little harbour, including Dad's blue one, the *Patricia*. The fishermen were standing around, peering at the sky, waiting for the signal to set off the search from Brendan and Johnny. They followed in their boats while we stood around beating our blue hands together, hoping for some sign from the sea that our dad was alive, unable to believe that this was happening. Year in, year out, whatever the weather, Dad always came home to us.

The boats sat heavy as the fishermen scooped down into the water with their oars, combing and sifting, the fishermen leaning over the side, peering down, shadows from the light from their lamps falling on to the rumpled sea. After every couple of strokes they would stop, then resume, their boats bobbing around, their efforts painstakingly slow.

As morning broke, a group of neighbours came and stood by the water's edge to keep vigil with us. Paddy-The-Stacker lit a fire and we stood around it, praying silently while we waited. Time didn't matter. I wanted to be at the shore to face whatever was coming rather than to go home with no news for Mam. As the north wind swept over the grey beach I felt sure that this cruel, unpredictable sea had snatched our dad from us, and I wondered how I would break the news to Mam and what I would do if I were never to see him again.

As the sun broke through the clouds schoolchildren gathered round, fear on their pink faces as they prayed with Miss Smith. Nell from the grocery shop brought a pot of scalding sweet tea wrapped in newspaper, mugs, milk, and buttered soda bread. Every moment of waiting was like an hour.

'We'll sing a hymn,' someone suggested.

When the first of the boats finally returned, the fishermen filed past us, their eyes downcast.

'Have they found him?' Alice asked one of them hopefully.

'Not so far,' he said, shaking his head doubtfully.

The boats returned one by one, the same forlorn expression on the faces of the fishermen.

As soon as Sheerin's boat struck the shore Alice and I ran down, breathless, pushing in front. A cry rang round the cold foreshore as Brendan and Johnny lifted a limp body off the boat, and carried it up the beach past the praying women and silent men, and laid it on the sand. Shivering with fear, we ran to the spot that revealed the dear face of our dad, his staring eyes as soulless as a dead fish.

'Dad!' I screamed, and fell on my knees to touch his face. It was cold as the grave, and white, a tuft of sodden hair fallen over his brow. I could smell the sharp death-smell of him, and was horrified by it.

'He's dead,' Johnny said, kneeling beside me, and putting his arm tight around me.

'No!' Alice's scream rent the air above me. Johnny caught her as she collapsed on to the sand. 'I can't bear to think of him dying out there all by himself,' she sobbed.

'Shh,' he said, stroking her matted hair.

I resolved to keep hold of myself for her sake, while all around us the women wept and prayed in low voices.

Gently, the Sheerins lifted Dad on to their horse and cart and brought him home, the rest of us trudging behind, the sky falling down on us, the cries of the seagulls following us all the way up from the white whirling bay. It began to rain heavily. The horse trotted along, splashing us.

In the village, neighbours came out of their doors on either side of the street, weeping. They followed us on our path of grief into our hushed yard where Mam was waiting, still hopeful that Dad would walk in. In the blowing yard, the wind dancing around her, she came to meet us full of chatter. A terrible silence followed as she peered upon the cart, her fist crammed into her mouth, like a child, to stifle the piercing scream that wrenched the air when she spotted Dad's lifeless body.

Brendan Sheerin jumped down and went to her. 'I'm sorry Pat, it's a desperate —' he began, but was silenced by the next roar that ripped from her, making the windowpanes tremble, before she collapsed against him like a rag doll. He grabbed hold of her and edged her towards the wall as he helped her inside.

Everything in the warm kitchen – from the familiar kettle that sang on the range, to the clock over the door – looked strange, as we walked past it to Mam and Dad's bedroom. Johnny and Brendan laid Dad gently down on his bed. Mam pulled the blankets over him and spread her fingers on his dull eyes. Smoothing back his hair, she bent down to kiss his forehead. In the flame of the candle he looked as if he was asleep.

I stood gazing at the slack face, put my fingertips on the gash on the side of his forehead, and couldn't believe that he had gone. I held the hand that had held my hand, and guided me along throughout my childhood. As my fingers tingled with the bone-chilling cold, I realised that he really was dead.

During the wake that followed, I left the bedroom so as not to hear the keening of the old women. In the kitchen, as I made tea for neighbours, I could hardly bear the long, agonising recounting of the hapless tale among them.

That night, a commotion broke out as a policeman arrived with Ed and kept his hand on Ed's shoulder as he led him into the house. Ed wept silently with Mam, while the neighbours surrounded the policeman with exclamations of horror at the way that he guarded him at a time like this.

As Brendan Sheerin called for order, Alice and I crept into our bedroom and sat whispering to fill the empty space. When Alice finally fell asleep, exhausted, I gazed out of the window at the barn in the shadow of the dark trees, and the church spire beyond it under the stars. Everywhere was ghostly. There were ghosts in the corners of fields; the trees were cluttered with spirits. The hunt for Dad was over and our world was thrown upside down. I lay awake all that night, listening to the sound of racking sobs. It felt like the saddest night in the world.

In the morning, I woke up thinking that it was only a dream. Dad was alive. Any minute now he would be up and calling me to help with the milking. But it wasn't a dream. The reality was in Mam's slumped shoulders as she sat by her bed, and the three candles that were burning, their flame dancing around the room. 'These candles mustn't be blown out.' She spoke like somebody reciting a poem that she'd learned by heart. Her skin was glazed, her face as waxy as the candles. Her eyes were wide and staring into the flame, she seemed locked into herself.

For the next couple of days, everything seemed suspended in air. Seated at the head of our kitchen table, Aunt Mabel took charge and made all the funeral arrangements. There was no ease from pain and sorrow as we went about on tiptoe preparing for it.

★   ★   ★

On the morning of the funeral, I kept my eyes on the coffin as it was lifted into the horse-drawn hearse. Dad's last journey took him down the hill past the shut-up shops, and up the path of the church, past graves and leafless trees, us walking silently behind him. The neighbours stood in the arch of the door and made the sign of the cross as the coffin was carried across the cobblestones and into the church, the call of a bird breaking the eerie silence.

After the funeral all the neighbours gathered round, comforting Mam as the coffin was lowered into the ground. People glanced at us, then glanced away as we walked out of the gates. Brendan and Johnny Sheerin, dressed in black suits, escorted us home – the whole village stopping to talk to us on the way.

It was strange coming back to the drawn curtains and the smell of stale whiskey and stout that had been drunk at the wake. Alice and I made tea and passed around sandwiches and sweet cake that the neighbours had brought.

After they had gone, Mam sat listless and sad. There wasn't an ounce of energy in her. Aunt Mabel sat in Dad's chair by the range, opposite her.

'What are you going to do, Pat? You can't run the farm on your own.'

Mam bowed her head. 'My task now is to care for my poor fatherless children and hope for the best.'

Aunt Mabel said, 'I think it might be a good idea

to sell up and to move in with me.' She looked to me for support.

'You're not expecting me to move into a town full of strangers,' Mam protested. 'How would we live? What would I do?'

'You could help out in the shop. I was only saying to Ellie the other day that I don't know anyone other than myself who can sew as good as you.'

A pleased expression passed fleetingly over Mam's face. 'I'm not young any more,' she said. 'I'm a forty-year-old woman with four children and another on the way. I'd only be a burden on you, Mabel,' she sighed. 'Why did God have to take him!' She crushed her rosary beads in her hands, a signal that it was the end of the matter for the time being.

Most of the time Mam stayed in her bedroom with the curtains drawn, as if by venturing out she'd lose sight of Dad's memory. In shock and grief she would kneel before her little statue of the Virgin Mary in that airless room, begging for explanations from the smiling chalk face. She lay with her eyes fixed on the photograph of Dad on their wedding day. Dad, handsome and smiling, with his hand aloft as if he were waving. Gazing at him she said, 'I remember the day we got married as if it were yesterday: I, in my lovely white dress and fine plumes on my hat that Mabel sent me from America. Your dad said that I looked like a queen.' I put my arms around her, wanting to comfort her, but I didn't know what to say so I just held her. I wanted everything to be as it had been, knowing that it never could be.

The fields were empty and silent. The sheep, in their pens, clung together, their heavy fleeces keeping them warm. The cows in the barn were quiet. The hens in the yard looked awkward and sad, as if they were afraid to squawk. Often I'd find Mam standing in the yard, listening to the rustle of the wind. Any noise at all – the flash of a rook across the back field or the sound of wind over the hills – would set her off in an agitated state. She'd snap at Shep for no reason. He, in turn, would snap at the hens, or hide in the barn, his big brown eyes mournful.

When kind-hearted neighbours with sad faces came to drink tea with her, Alice and Lucy would hide in their bedroom and play together, not finding the kitchen the comforting place that it used to be. I spent my time with the animals, and kept out of the way too.

In the evenings Alice and Lucy would hover around Mam, trying to comfort her. They would pull a rug around her, prop cushions behind her head, and tell her about school, even read their essays to her. Anything to distract her. When she went to her room, Lucy would follow her and lie down on the bed beside her protectively.

Each day I collected the eggs, wading through the

nests, sending the hens flying in all directions, desperate to get as many as possible, then I cycled to the town on Mam's black-framed bicycle to sell them, the straw basket secured tightly to the handlebars.

'How's your mother?' Nell in the grocer's would ask in a low voice every time I went into the shop. 'Not too good,' I'd say, and she'd shake her head sadly. I'd cycle home heavy-hearted from all the sympathy that was poured on me by well-meaning people, and place the money into the palm of Mam's hand.

And there was the constant cleaning, as though my life depended on it, to prove to Mam that it was possible to carry on. But she never seemed to notice. Sometimes I would find her leaning on the window ledge, watching the road, and I'd want to pull her away and hand her a bucketful of grain to feed the hens. But I didn't have the heart to.

As time went on, the house became a dark, dreary place with the curtains permanently drawn. At night, Mam's sobs resounded around the house as if she were being wrenched asunder.

She began to wander out at night. We'd wake to find her coming in, closing the door from the yard. We'd try to stay awake to stop her wandering off again, but mostly we fell asleep.

The winter days were cold and dreary. The rain cracked down like gunfire, then for the rest of November it poured in a never-ending sheet flooding the fields. The wind moaned and muttered from dark until dawn. It rattled the shutters and drove the rain beneath the doors.

'The walls are falling down around you. You'll have to leave here,' Aunt Mabel said, when she came to visit us. Mam shaped her lips to protest, but no words came out.

Policemen patrolled the lanes on horseback after some of the local men were found in possession of arms. I ran to Sheerin's to find out if Ed was in any danger. Johnny assured me that he'd slipped away in the nick of time. I was grateful for his assurance.

Lucy made Christmas cards in school and brought them home to send to no one. Christmas was not celebrated that year.

One morning, after milking, I got back to find that Mam wasn't in the kitchen. Her bedroom was empty. 'Mam!' I called out to her. There was no answer. I went back out to search for her and eventually found her sitting in the sheltered cove by Dad's boat, feeding the seagulls from stale bread she had in the pocket of her old gabardine coat.

'Mam!' She didn't seem to hear me. I sat down beside her on the wet stones.

'They say that seagulls are the ghosts of the drowned,' she said.

I looked at one of the greedy white birds, its feathers

ruffling in the wind, its watchful eyes on the bread, and couldn't see a connection.

Shyly she said, 'I came to say goodbye to the boat. That's the last we'll see of it. It's going to the breaker's yard tomorrow.'

'But why not sell it? It's in perfect condition. You'd get a good price for it.'

'No one would buy it. It's unlucky, they say.'

'Oh Mam!' I put my arm around her. She was chilled to the bone. 'Come on home, you'll get pneumonia sitting here.' I took her hand and pulled her up. She walked beside me tensely, her coat billowing around her.

Once inside, I sat her down and removed her swamped boots. 'You can't go wandering off like that, Mam,' I said to her.

She didn't seem to hear me, instead she said, 'I must have covered every inch of this beauty spot on the walks I used to take with your dad when I first came here.' She blinked back tears. I followed her gaze past the fields to the sea in the distance, smooth as glass, the sun lazing over it. 'Your dad said it was the one way to get to know a place, and he was right.'

I looked out at the empty fields and wondered that life could continue without him.

Without warning, white hawthorn blossoms appeared on the hedgerows; gold ribbons of gorse trailed through the fields, brightening them and lifting our spirits. Birds flew round the trees, building their nests. New shoots appeared in the fields. Early daffodils raised their heads above the frozen earth. The air was light, the animals were restless. Spring was on its way and with it came the lambing season.

The fishermen were back working in the fields. I thought that I could deliver the lambs on my own because I'd seen Dad and Ed do it plenty of times. Also, I was taller and stronger than the previous year. But when I led our first pregnant ewe into the barn I stood, helpless, as the poor ewe heaved and moaned; I didn't know what to do. As soon as Alice came home from school I sent her to fetch Johnny, who ran across two fields to help me.

Catching sight of the moaning ewe, Johnny rolled up his sleeves and gently eased out the lamb with expert hands. He wiped the coating of film from it with a flour bag, and stood it on its legs. It jumped into life. Panting, he sat back on his hunkers to rest, sweat dripping from his brow.

Each day, he continued to deliver the lambs. As soon as they were born I'd clean them up, spread fresh straw around them, and place them under their mothers to be fed. Late into the night, I'd watch over them. I took twin lambs that weren't thriving from their mother and brought them indoors, where Alice and Lucy bottle-fed them by the range and cradled them like babies.

All in all, we had ten lambs to fatten up. When they

were ready to sell, Johnny piled them into his cart on market day and off he drove with them. When he returned to give the money to Mam she offered to pay him for his help, but he refused to take it, and assured her that soon I'd be a fully-fledged farmer and well able to manage on the farm.

'I can't do it all on my own,' I protested to him out in the yard.

'Ellie, I can help with the ploughing.'

'No thanks.'

'Why not?'

'Because unless Ed comes home soon and takes over, there won't be a living to be made here.'

Johnny gave me a peculiar look. 'There isn't much chance of that happening at the present time.'

'How do you know? Have you got news of Ed?' I asked eagerly.

He nodded. 'He's hurt.'

My hands flew to my mouth. 'Where is he?'

'I can't say. I'm sworn to secrecy.'

'You *have* to tell me. I want to talk to him, find out everything that's happening to him.'

'All right, but you have to keep it a secret. You mustn't tell your mam. If she finds out that he's in the vicinity she'll be anxious.'

Together we went back to his farm. Ed was in Sheerin's loft, sitting on a makeshift bed in a corner, a trench coat over his knees, a pile of maps beside him.

'Ed, what's happened to you?'

Tilting his head back he said, 'I got hurt.'

'What were you doing?'

'Never mind. Listen, Ellie, I'm safe here. Johnny and Brendan are taking care of me,' he said, limping around the loft uneasily. 'Anyway, I'll be leaving here shortly.'

'Where are you off to?'

He gave a slow smile. 'I can't say – but don't worry about me, I'll be all right,' he assured me, though I wasn't convinced.

I walked back to the house in the twilight, scared of what was going to happen to him.

As time went on, Mam seemed to be more sorrowful than ever. One day she said, 'Ellie, I can't go on like this. I can't manage without your father.'

'We'll leave here, move in with Aunt Mabel. Start afresh,' I said.

Mam shook her head and turned away, but I cycled to Aunt Mabel to explain the worsening situation and to ask her to come and talk sense into her.

Aunt Mabel returned with me and got straight to the point. 'You're almost eight months pregnant, Pat; you can't stay here any longer,' she said, looking around in frustration.

Mam's jaw jutted out. 'What would I do in the town? I don't know anyone there any more,' she protested.

'You can help out in the shop, potter round the garden.'

'And what about my baby when it's born?'

'Peggy and I will help you take care of it, and you can always come back later on.'

Mam shook her head. 'No, Mabel, your house isn't big enough for all of us.'

Mabel paused. I think you should send Ellie to America – to stay with Jack. She'll have a much better chance of an education over there. Let's face it, she's not cut out for farm work . . . and Jack's our brother – he'll be more than happy to put her up . . . Perhaps Alice, too? It wouldn't be for ever . . .'

Mam shook her head. 'I know that, but I'd find it too hard to part with her.'

'I want to go too,' Alice said.

'Oh Mam! Please can we go?' we begged her.

Aunt Mabel looked at Alice. 'You'd be a nice companion for Mary-Pat,' she said encouragingly, adding, 'Mary-Pat is Jack's daughter – she's about your age. I think.' Jack thinks it sounds like a good plan anyway . . .'

Shocked, Mam turned to her. 'You've asked him already?'

'Yes, and he's agreed to give both the girls an education in return for light housework. Then we'd have only Lucy to look after until the new baby arrives. We'd easily manage.'

41

Mam shifted uneasily in her chair. 'But . . . Where would I get the money to pay for their passage?' she said doubtfully.

'I'll pay their fare,' Aunt Mabel said. 'They can pay me back when they've made it out there.' She winked at us behind Mam's back.

'But who'll take care of the farm until Ed comes home?' Mam asked.

'The Sheerins will keep an eye on it for you. You can sell the cattle. Ed can buy more when he returns,' Aunt Mabel said.

'I suppose it would be the sensible thing to do.'

Aunt Mabel straightened her back like a general's. 'That's settled then. I'll write to Uncle Jack and Aunt Sally. I know Miss Smith will give the girls good references.'

Mam opened her mouth to protest, but no words came out. Aunt Mabel went and put her arms around her. 'You can always come back after the baby's born and you're stronger,' she assured her.

'I suppose so.' I could see that Mam didn't have the energy to argue with her.

Brisk and businesslike, she left to make all the arrangements for our move to town.

'So, we're leaving our home,' Mam said to me after Aunt Mabel had gone.

I rested my hand on hers. 'We mustn't be sad. Dad wouldn't want it.'

'You're right. We mustn't be sad any more.' Mam smiled for the first time since Dad's death. Her wedding ring flashed brightly as she moved her hand across the window, as if wiping it clean to see what wasn't there.

I followed her gaze to the orange and yellow hens pecking around the yard and said, 'I wonder if Brendan will take them for the time being.'

The light from the setting sun threw shadows across her taut cheeks and emphasised the smudges beneath her eyes. Running her hand through her hair, she said, 'We must take a last walk across the fields.'

Early one morning Mam said, 'Come on, let's get started on the packing.' Her dress rustled as she raised her arms to take down the china ornaments from the mantlepiece to pack them in cardboard boxes. In her bedroom she reluctantly placed her precious candlesticks in her good linen sheets, pressing them down with the sweep of her hands. Then she packed all Dad's clothes into a flour sack and took them away, while I got started on our bedroom. When she returned later there were tears on her cheeks.

'What did you do with them?'

'I gave them to Nell to take to the workhouse.' Her voice shook.

Without warning, tears spilled down my cheeks, the realisation of his death hitting home, with every trace of him now gone. Mam held me tight while I cried.

Later, I went to over to Sheerin's. Johnny was digging up beet for cattle-feed when I got there. 'I have something to tell you,' I said to him.

He stuck his fork in the ground and looked at me, waiting. 'Mam and Lucy are going to live with Aunt Mabel, and Alice and me are going to America to our Uncle Jack. It's all decided.' The words tumbled out with my excitement at the prospect of a new life in New York.

'So, you've got your wish. You're going away,' he said solemnly.

'Yes. I can't wait. And I want you to tell Ed the news if you see him.'

'I'll do that. The big city, eh? You'll miss the fields and the trees, and you'll miss your friends,' he warned.

'I know that, but we'll have a better chance over there, and when I'm working I'll be able to send money home to Mam.'

'And when you come back you'll be too grand for us.'

'No, I won't,' I said stubbornly.

Slowly, we made our way back across the fields as the sun sank behind the trees in a great fiery ball, bathing them in a gold light. Outside our cottage, Johnny said, 'No matter where you go I'll always think of you as being here.'

'This is my place,' I agreed. To lighten the mood I said, 'Some day I might come back to visit you.'

'Promise me that you will,' Johnny said.

'I promise,' I said.

★ ★ ★

On market day, Johnny and I drove our few cows to the cattle market in Garrystown to sell them. The market was packed with rugged farmers in tweed caps, who gathered around the square eyeing the cattle in their pens. One farmer ran an expert hand over the flanks of one of our cows while he argued with Johnny over the price. I stayed watchful, while Johnny bargained casually with him as if he had all the time in the world and money wasn't important. A deal was struck. The farmer spat into the palm of his hand before shaking hands with us to seal it. We celebrated the success of the sale in Rafferty's pub with a bottle of lemonade for me, and a pint of stout for him, the money safe in my coat pocket.

Mam was waiting for us with a dinner of bacon and cabbage. When I handed her the money, her eyes widened with gratitude. 'That's more than I expected,' she said thankfully.

When Johnny was leaving, I walked out to the yard with him. 'It was a good day's work,' he said.

'You've been a good friend to us, Johnny, and I'm grateful to you. I've relied on your opinion on almost everything since Dad died,' I said to him.

'You're important in my life too, Ellie.' With a sigh he said, 'I'll miss you.'

I looked up into his eyes.

'I'll miss you too,' I assured him as together we gazed

up at the moon, a thin silver disc casting its magic light all around us, for the last time.

By the time we were ready to leave, there were boxes everywhere. It had taken us a week to pack up and less than an hour for Brendan and Johnny Sheerin to pile our belongings on to their cart and take them to one of their dry barns to store them.

Mam shut the door of each room for the last time and moved swiftly away from the cottage, the emptiness too much for her.

Aunt Mabel drove us to Garrystown in her pony and trap, an ostrich plume in her new tartan hat. At the gate, I turned to look back at our cottage and thought I saw Dad standing in a dark corner of the yard.

Peggy had prepared our dinner and Aunt Mabel insisted that Mam have a glass of wine. For the first time since Dad's death Mam was cheerful, babbling away until Aunt Mabel finally coaxed her up to bed.

The next day, Alice and I began preparations for our trip to New York and our new life.

Four

Mam, wrapped into her shawl, Lucy beside her, stood at the gate silently watching us go, one hand raised in farewell, the other wiping back her tears, the sadness of our parting etched on her face. Aunt Mabel, next to her, waved and waved. At the corner I looked back, and in that brief moment I felt their loneliness, before the excitement of the journey took hold of me.

Mam had risen at dawn to cook us breakfast, and had made us ham sandwiches for the journey and a stout bottle of milk each, while Aunt Mabel fussed around with the last of our packing. Enveloped in our new coats and our new felt hats we felt grand sitting in the trap behind Johnny on that chill spring morning, our cloth bags on our laps, our cardboard suitcase behind us. All the restless worry of waiting and watching the road for the postman, for the word that would give us permission to go, was over. We were on our way.

We passed the dark windows of the empty school and the white statue of the Virgin Mary as we went on down the narrow road through the slumbering fields under the plum-coloured mountain, past the sea shining innocently in the sunlight, shadows of the clouds moving above it.

Once on the road for Cobh, the horse clopped along to the tinkling sound of the chapel bell. 'I'm glad to be leaving,' Alice said.

'So am I,' I said, looking back at our sleeping village. We were free at last, and the world was ours.

The little town of Cobh was layered with coloured houses that wound around the headland. Above their sloping roofs stood the majestic cathedral, supreme as a king on a throne, its dark shadow slanting across the shops below. In the harbour, our ship, the SS *Carolina*, loomed – a dominating presence in the tiny town, a queue already forming beneath its huge, white hull. Whole families were grouped together under the long-roofed pier, full of echoing shouts. Men clutched baskets and boxes, while their wives guarded children who ran around excitedly.

At the door marked 'Departure' Johnny took my hands in his warm ones and held them for a long time as he said goodbye. 'Be sure to write to me about all the nice things that happen to you over there – even the not so nice – won't you?' he said.

'Oh, I will. I'll tell you all about college and what I'm learning,' I said enthusiastically.

Bending close to touch my hair, he said softly, 'You'll be fancied by all the Yanks.'

'Don't be silly,' I laughed, delighted at the compliment.

'It's true. You're beautiful, Ellie. It's not just me that thinks it, either – everyone says so.'

'Thank you, Johnny.'

'You won't forget us?' Glancing up I saw that there were tears in his eyes.

'How could I?' I looked into his face, memorising every inch and every line of it. He leaned closer. 'You'll come back one day, won't you?' he said, his eyes soft, almost pleading.

'I promise I will,' I said earnestly, meaning every word of it.

'If you don't, I'll come searching for you,' he smiled.

Tearfully, we said goodbye.

Prior to boarding the ship we had to undergo a health inspection to detect disease or illness, grounds for denying us entrance into the United States. Then we were herded briskly aboard. At the top of the gangway, two stewards directed us to the quarterdeck where, under the stern gaze of an officer, we waited to wave goodbye to Johnny. All around us people held on to each other stiffly as they waved, their faces set in farewell. It seemed as if the whole town had turned out to witness our departure.

A gong sounded. The gangplanks were removed as the

crowds behind the barrier waved and called. There was a loud, mournful sound of the horn, and the vibration of the ship as it slowly pulled away from the dock. People ran to catch a last frenzied glimpse of us. There was desperation in the way they stood at the edge of the pier, waving and calling out, their last goodbyes in sad pursuit of the churning noise of the propellers.

'We're moving,' Alice cried.

I threw my hat in the air, caught it again, and plonked it back on my head, laughing with delight. As the blurred houses along the waterfront slid by, we caught sight of Johnny at the edge of the pier. We waved and waved to him, our coats flapping against our legs, our handkerchiefs fluttering as the sea raced by, until the town was just a spire rising out of the misty shore.

The ship picked up speed and ploughed swiftly forward, its diesel engines pounding and throbbing as it headed eastward. In the darkening evening the sky took on a delicate shade of duck-egg blue that reflected on the water and merged into the horizon. Gulls flew high above us, their wings dipping like silver blades, their cries lonely. They stayed with us until the shore was just a long charcoal line of rocks receding into the mountains. When the wind rose, whipping them homeward, they glided off into the curve of the bay before disappearing altogether, leaving nothing but an immense grey sea with waves of green foam.

The vibration of the ship in motion made Alice feel queasy.

'Do you want to go downstairs?' I asked her.

'No, I like it here,' she said bravely, looking around, her vision of the world narrowed down to an aft deck full of people.

This was the beginning of our adventure. For the first time I realised that I was leaving Ireland, perhaps for good. In that instant I felt home clutch at my heart like fingers of steel. I could smell its soil, feel the softness of its grass, see its trees heavy with leaves.

The sun set, leaving crimson trails the colour of blood. I thought of my poor, bruised land, recalling the battle cries of the farmers, and the outbursts of young men in the local hall, their voices choked off by their dreams. I remembered the sound of the gunfire ricocheting across the hills, deafening us to the chime of the church bells, and Father Slattery preaching of hellfire and brimstone in an attempt to put the fear of God into all those in revolt against the new government.

I thought of Ed and his secrets, and bid him a silent goodbye as I guiltily turned my back on him.

The Fastnet lighthouse flashed its guiding beams across our watery path. Trails of smoke from the dirty cream funnel rose up into the air as the great sweep of heaving Atlantic Ocean rolled to an invisible horizon, revealing more distance than I could ever have imagined. This was the real sea. There was one star in the sky. I thought of that summer night when they brought Dad home. There had been no stars out that night.

The wind was as sharp as a knife, wrinkling the water. Gripping the iron rail, Alice shivered. I put my arm around her. 'You're not to be afraid,' I said.

'Oh, I'm not. Not for a second, I promise you,' she said. 'I'm glad to be here.' There was gratitude in her voice.

It grew dark. A young steward came over to us and said, with the air of a patient nanny, 'I think you should go below, find yourselves a cosy spot. I'll help you with your luggage.'

He escorted us through a freshly painted white door, down narrow steel steps to our dingy quarters in steerage. It was a huge, cold, dimly lit cellar, smelling of unwashed clothes, below the water line. There was no fresh air, no sky, only sea to look out at, and the throbbing of the engines to deafen us. Families sat together amid their belongings. Most of them were seasick. Some of them were weeping, bemoaning the hole we were expected to live in for the voyage.

'I didn't want to leave,' one woman said to another.

'We had to go,' her husband said softly.

'We'll never go back,' she said, with an air of exhaustion. 'Not the way things are.' There was hoarse agreement all round.

I wanted to think that they were wrong, but I was too young and too full of my own dream to understand the full implications of their remarks. The scale of Ireland's troubles and its poverty had no real meaning for me.

Stewards separated single men and women. Alice and I were assigned to a specific sleeping location. In the dormitory we picked out our bunk rack, made of steel pipe with fabric stretched over the framework. There, among the watertanks and exposed pipes, amid the murmuring, half-stifled coughing, heavy breathing, and the frightened moans of a pregnant woman nearby, we ate our sandwiches and settled down for the night. There was no pillow, just one grey blanket each. Things were not going to be easy. Finally, cigarettes were stubbed out, the coughing and shuffling died down, and there was silence – except for the occasional moan – as everybody settled down to sleep. Trapped in this noisy, congested, smelly place, with no privacy, and with the sound of the sea hitting the sides of the ship making such a racket, it was difficult to close our eyes.

'I can't sleep,' Alice whispered. 'My stomach is rolling. Do you feel it too?'

'Yes, we'll settle down soon as we get used to it.' I put my arm around her, pulled her to me. 'We'll have a great time when we get to America, and we'll be much better off – and happier.'

'We'll never fight any more about silly things. We'll never be mean to one another again.'

'No never.'

'And we'll always be together?' she asked.

Even as we cuddled up together, I knew she was feeling the same sheer isolation that I was feeling.

Next morning, we were up before the other passengers were awake. Alice felt sick so we went in search of fresh air. Silently, we climbed the stairway and ducked past crates of cargo and lifeboats as the ship rode on the water, slicing its way through the yielding sea, leaving a line of steam trailing behind it.

It was cold on deck, with a spray from the waves like rain. 'Let's go back,' I said.

'No, I want to explore,' she said.

There was no one about so, daringly, we jumped over the chain that separated us from the second-class deck and sneaked across the forbidden territory to portside. We walked along the deck. Pushing along the deck we headed aft, the wind on our faces bringing with it the taste of salt and the smell of tar, disinfectant and cooking that made Alice feel nauseous again. I took her back and helped her into bed.

'You'd better stay here,' I said, straightening her blanket. 'I'll bring you some breakfast later on.'

A woman gave her an arrowroot biscuit and told her that if she ate it she'd feel better. While she slept, I returned to the deck and explored it as much as I could until I heard a rush of footsteps, and women and children came tumbling out, excitedly calling out to one another, invading the place.

I went below to breakfast and queued with the others for tea and thick slices of bread and butter, which I brought back to Alice. She ate a little of her share, hunched down in our corner.

Later, feeling better, she played a game of Beggar My Neighbour with two girls, Hannah and Kathleen, who were about her own age. I joined in.

That evening, one of the men who had brought his violin with him, played sad songs into the night.

On the second day, Alice was still as sick as a dog and stayed in bed. In the afternoon I went off exploring, forcing my way through the bins and the smoky atmosphere of the funnels, up two flights of iron stairs to the first-class deck. The disdainful eyes of the jewel-adorned women on deckchairs, with their well-dressed, distinguished husbands by their sides, slid over me as I walked along. I looked seaward, and let my hair blow over my face to hide my embarrassment.

Further on, elegant girls in cream and white, and wearing smart hats and strings of pearls, exchanged amusing gossip with exotic-looking boys, their deep-red lips creased in wide, open smiles. For a moment I forgot myself and imagined that I was one of them, dressed in silk, grandly sipping tea. Among them was a slim, pale, dark-haired girl, with a sweet face. She caught my eye and smiled at me, and I smiled back gratefully. She came over to me.

'Are you all right?' she asked.

Shocked at being spoken to, I nodded mutely.

The girl held out her hand. 'I'm Violet Kelleher,' she said. 'What's your name?'

'Eleanor,' I said, a little nervously, taking her hand briefly.

'Are you travelling alone?' she asked.

'No, I'm with my sister, she's not feeling very well.'

'I'm sorry to hear that,' she said.

She told me that she was on her way back to Boston with her cousin Zak, who was accompanying her, having spent a holiday in London. She kindly invited me to join them for tea.

'I'm afraid I can't. I'm travelling steerage,' I said, disappointed.

'Don't worry,' she smiled. 'You'll be my guest.'

My hunger and curiosity triumphed over my better judgement, and I followed her to the dining room. The 'fun-loving' girls were there. I could see the look of surprise on their hard faces when they spotted me. Violet introduced me, explained to them that I was alone because my sister was ill.

I managed to hide my feelings of inferiority, and kept my poise when a brisk waitress with a frilly cap glided noiselessly around us serving plates of cucumber sandwiches and dainty, iced cakes on three-tiered cake stands. Eating slowly and self-consciously, I exclaimed how delicious the sandwiches tasted to show my appreciation, and noticed the amused glances of the girls. One of them leaned forward and, cupping her hand over her mouth, whispered into the ear of her companion, who burst out laughing, and I blushed. Seeing this Violet said, 'They're giving a little performance for the boys here, trying to attract their attention.' She laughed. 'They're really only interested in their social lives.' The boys in question were too far away to hear what the joke was, but they responded to each burst of hilarity by laughing back.

While we nibbled the delicate cakes Violet chatted on, telling me about her family. In return I told her about Mam and Lucy and Aunt Mabel's shop and the life I'd left behind. I was about to tell her about Dad's death but I suddenly found myself choking in the rush of tears. Mistaking my distress for homesickness, Violet said quickly, 'Come on, let's go and find Zak. I can't think where he's got to.' We excused ourselves and left the table. I followed her out on to the deck. 'There he is,' she said, smiling.

I turned to see a young man walking towards us. He was tall and handsome with golden hair that flopped over his forehead. He had high cheekbones and deep-set amber eyes. In a dark suit, a crisp white shirt, and striped tie, he looked elegant, like a film star.

'I waited for you in the dining room,' Violet said to him.

With a carefree smile he said, 'I'm not hungry. Haven't found my sea legs yet.'

'Zak, may I introduce you to Miss Eleanor O'Rourke,' Violet said with great formality.

The wind blew his dark hair backwards and made his cheeks glow, as Zak subtly looked me up and down. I pushed back my hair and pulled my coat around me to hide my shabby frock beneath, regretting not putting on my best one.

'Miss O'Rourke, how do you do?' He shook my hand.

'Pleased to meet you, I'm sure.' I couldn't think of another thing to say so I took a step back, wishing I'd taken more care with my hair and put on a little of the lipstick Aunt Mabel had given me.

With a crooked grin, he said in a husky voice, 'And where are you heading for, Miss O'Rourke?'

'Call me Ellie. That's what my friends call me. I'm going to New York.' I faced out to sea too shy to look at him directly.

'Ellie,' he repeated, savouring the sound. 'You travelling alone?' His eyes on me were drawing me in.

'No, my sister is with me. She's not feeling well today.'

'I'm sorry to hear that. The sea is quite rough.' There was a small pause, before he went on. 'Do you have relatives in New York?'

'Yes, my uncle is meeting us.'

'Good.' There was something unusual in his expression as he stood looking at me.

I wanted to continue talking to him so I asked him about himself. Proudly, he told me about his good position in a bank in Boston. I told him that I was looking forward to completing my education and learning a craft.

'Great! I hope it works out well for you,' he said.

'Thank you.' I turned to Violet. 'I'd better be getting back to Alice,' I said.

'Come for afternoon tea again tomorrow. Bring Alice, if she's feeling better,' Violet suggested.

Alice was engrossed in a game of 'Fish' with her new friends, Kathleen and Hannah, when I got back to her. 'Where did you get to?' she asked.

'I made some new friends in first class,' I said excitedly.

'First class!'

'Yes, and they've invited us both for afternoon tea tomorrow, if you're feeling up to it. Oh, Alice, it'll be fun.'

The following afternoon was very windy, with high tides that made Alice feel even more unwell. She didn't feel up to coming to first class with me so I tucked the coarse blanket around her and, leaving her in the care of Kathleen and Hannah, I sneaked up on deck to meet Violet as arranged. I was surprised when Zak appeared alone.

'Violet is seasick. She sends her apologies,' he said warmly.

'Oh dear! That's a shame,' I said, nervous at being alone with a strange boy.

'We don't want to stand around here in the cold; let's take a stroll along the deck,' he said.

We strolled along as the wind picked up and the deck tilted from side to side as the ship rolled and creaked. With a violent lurch it pitched to one side. Startled, I lurched forward. Zak grabbed me and steadied me.

'Let's get out of here before the next big wave,' he said. We ducked down behind a lifeboat and sat there watching the dark banks of waves rushing by, their colour changing from wine-red to deep green as they streamed away. The first stars appeared in the sky. Fragments of a waltz blew out across the sea. Sea-spray dashed against the stern.

I bit my lip anxiously. 'I'm worried that I shall be caught up here by one of the stewards,' I admitted, looking around.

'Oh, don't concern yourself. You're with me,' Zak reassured me.

His face, in the wan light, was smooth as his eyes focused on me. We talked together. Zak was serious as he explained about being an only child, and the expectations his parents had for him. The ship lurched and he put his arm protectively around me. 'I wish they'd slow her up a bit in this storm,' he said, drawing me to him. It was pleasant sitting together above the fierce, mechanical pull of the engines, while Zak told me all about the sights he'd seen in London. It seemed so glamorous, and though in the back of my mind I remembered the countless warnings Aunt Mabel and Mam had given us about being alone with strange men, I didn't want to think about that now. I wanted to listen to Zak as he told me about his family in Boston.

'There's a tea dance tomorrow afternoon. Will you come?' he asked.

'I don't think I'd be allowed in.' I looked doubtfully at him.

'I'm sure Violet will be better by then, and you will be our guest,' he said with confidence.

The opportunity of spending time with him and his cousin was far too tempting to refuse. My heart raced ahead of my brain as I agreed to meet him the following afternoon.

When I returned to steerage I found Alice much brighter. When I told her my exciting news, she was happy for me.

'What'll you wear?' she asked. Panic-stricken, I looked through our case for the white muslin frock Aunt Mabel had made me for the Harvest Festival and tried it on.

'What do you think?' I asked Alice, as I did a twirl.

'It's lovely,' she assured me.

'I'm so nervous,' I confided to her.

'Go on with you. You'll be all right once you get there. You'll have a great time.'

That night, I lay awake on my lumpy mattress, too excited to sleep, as I thought of the forthcoming tea dance . . . and Zak.

Five

The setting sun dominated the sea as Zak and Violet escorted me to the tea dance in the dining room, where the atmosphere of luxury bowled me over. The leaves of potted palms swayed back and forth, casting shadows over tables draped with woven embroidered cloths. Waiters were serving piled-high plates while an orchestra wooed us with happy tunes. I stood in the doorway, shifting my weight from one foot to the other, tempted to run back to steerage and Alice.

'You'll like it, it's fun,' Violet said, taking my arm and guiding me across the floor. Wishing it were longer, I pulled down my frock as I went.

The girls from the previous day were very grand. Decked out in their silver and gold flapper dresses, with their wraps and feather boas, they looked very stylish. They were talking to the boys.

'I asked Eleanor to join us,' Violet told them.

'Hello again,' one of them said, her eyes travelling up and down my body.

For all their apparent gaiety I could feel that they

were suspicious of me. I was not one of them. I tried to swallow my tea.

'Eleanor.' Zak nudged me. I turned round so fast that I almost knocked the plate of sandwiches he was holding out to me on to the floor.

'Sorry!' I said flustered.

'No harm done.' His hand brushed mine reassuringly. 'Would you like a champagne cocktail instead of that awful tea?' he asked me.

'I don't drink,' I said blushing. But Zak smiled.

'Just a drop . . .' he said, handing me a small glassful.

I could feel his eyes on me as I took a tentative sip. It made the whole of me feel warm, and it tasted quite nice. I took another sip, and another. With each sip I felt more relaxed. My nerves subsided, and suddenly those snooty rich girls were far less intimidating. After a while it seemed that nothing could spoil my evening. I paid the rich girls no more attention and instead concentrated on Zak, admiring his perfect skin and his hands, which were beautifully smooth. He had obviously never known a hard day's manual work in his life.

English and American couples sat so correctly together at nearby tables and talked of touring capitals and parties that I was glad I wasn't among them. I caught a look from one of them that temporarily made me uneasy, but I turned quickly away, and when the band started to play and Zak asked me to dance I jumped up too eagerly.

My feet didn't feel too steady as I followed him across the polished floor to the rustle of silk and satin gowns. As we twirled to the heavenly music, my inhibitions were ousted and my thoughts were only of the good-looking young man who was leading me with such grace and perfect rhythm. I lifted my head and met his gaze. He smiled his reassuring smile.

The next dance was the tango. After a stumble or two, I remembered Aunt Mabel's instructions to let myself be led. We swayed to its beat, Zak's hand in the small of my back, firm. At the interval a black woman in a beaded cerise dress, sang. *There's One Thing That I've Got, It's My Man* in a soft yearning voice. When she sang '*Sugar Blues*', everyone joined in the refrain. I didn't know the words but I didn't care. I was happy. All the worries of leaving home slowly melted away. I lost myself in the enchantment of the song and the dance. I was having the time of my life.

The band broke into a quickstep, setting my feet on fire. Arms flailing, heels kicking, we flew round and round, the music rushing us along with its tingling rhythm. With Zak leading, we managed difficult pivots and turns that Aunt Mabel would have been proud of, our heels hitting the floor in perfect harmony. I'd never realised that dancing could be so full of joy. This was what I'd left home for. I felt wonderful. With a flourish the music stopped. In the burst of clapping that followed, Zak ushered me out through the French door.

Under the string of lanterns that stretched along the deck, his face glowed. 'Ellie! You're so lovely,' he said.

'Thank you,' I giggled, clutching the railing. Awkward with this compliment I stood tongue-tied looking out to sea, marvelling at the fact that there was no life anywhere in its entire expanse except on the ship. It was full of life, with music floating out from the ballroom and people gathered in little groups, talking.

A fingernail of moon hovered above us, as he took my hands in his and drew me to him. His dark eyes glittered. 'I mean it, you look like an angel.' He leaned towards me and, to the strains of violins, I found myself being kissed under a veil of stars. Until that moment I'd been keeping myself at bay. But, caught up in the beauty of the night, and glad of the darkness, I let myself go, and kissed him back in a moment of complete response.

My eyes were still closed when I felt feet skirt around me. A shape passed by me, breaking the spell. I opened them to see the big, flat face of a steward thrusting itself between us. There was cold displeasure in the arch of his shoulders as he turned inquisitively to Zak. 'Sir, I don't know if you are aware that this passenger is from steerage? This area of the ship is out of bounds to her.' His breath blew warm and insultingly into my face.

'But she's with me,' Zak protested to no avail.

Giving me a lowering look, the steward gripped my arm and ordered me to follow him. Cold with humiliation, I was escorted through the ballroom to the wail of the tango, leaving Zak dumbstruck.

All eyes turned to me, with what I was sure was scandalised horror. As we passed the lavender-haired ladies, I could hear myself being distinguished as 'that steerage girl' by a woman in full evening dress, with a silly tiara on her head and a crushed orchid on her shoulder. I heard another one of them say scornfully, 'What is the world coming to, letting people of that class in here?' I tried not to look in their direction as I was shifted quickly by, taken below in stern silence.

As we came to the big doorway that led down to steerage, the steward left me with a warning not to stray from my quarters again. 'If I catch you up here again I'll report you,' he said. I backed in through the door, and stood alone and desolate in the darkness for a long time before I could find my bearings and my way back to Alice.

Tearfully, I lay in my bunk thinking of Zak, while somewhere above me the dance was still going on. I listened to the music, wondering how I might meet him and Violet again. Obviously, I couldn't go looking for them. From now on I would be fenced in.

'Hmm,' Alice said, next morning, when I told her what had happened. 'And here was me thinking you had them all fooled.'

'I wasn't trying to fool anybody.'

'Do you think you'll see Zak again?' she asked.

'I doubt it,' I said desolately. 'We'll be docking tomorrow.' I began folding my clothes carefully.

'You'd want to hurry up and think of some way of giving him your address in New York,' she said.

I hadn't thought of that. Now, suddenly realising its urgency, I knew that I'd have to see him again if only to give him my address.

The following day, as everyone was preparing to leave the ship, watched over by a steward, I waited my chance. With all the courage I could muster, I sneaked towards the chained-off iron steps.

'Where are you going?'

I looked up to see the same steward confronting me as I climbed the spiral stairs.

'I'm not feeling very well,' I said, and hung over the rail pretending to retch. He turned away shaking his head, leaving me with an undignified reminder of my inferior place. I decided not to give the sap another reason to belittle me, so I didn't stray from steerage again. I just hoped it wasn't the last I'd see of Zak.

I woke to the sound of someone shouting 'New York New York!' I was tired and grumpy at being disturbed because I was having a lovely dream about Zak. Not that I'd enjoyed the tedious journey, or the gasping spurts of the ship and the deep roll of the sea beneath it, but I'd grown used to it and was fearful of leaving its safety.

In the sharp first light we made our way up on to the deck as the ship looped round the bay and the Statue of Liberty rose out of the mist.

Bundled together, we stood on the upper deck as we sailed down the Hudson River past the gigantic green Statue of Liberty. As we entered the south channel of New York harbour someone pointed out Jamaica Bay and Coney Island. Tugboats appeared to guide us through the narrows into the bay past Staten Island and New Jersey to the west, Brooklyn to the east.

We sailed past freighters and festive steamboats with their tall slender smokestacks, awnings on their sun decks and big Stars and Stripes at their sterns, towards the harbour, our future assured in its glowing mouth. Out of the mist, we had our first glimpse of the Manhattan skyline with its proud skyscrapers: huge silhouettes that rose up into the clouds, their shadows rippling like flags on the motionless water.

Chains rattled over the side of the ship as it dropped anchor at Hudson River pier. As the first-class passengers waited to disembark, someone nudged my elbow. It was Zak and Violet.

'Ellie! We found you. We've been looking everywhere for you,' Violet said breathlessly. 'I thought we might not see you again.'

'Listen, I'm sorry about what happened. I didn't realise it would cause so much trouble for you,' Zak added kindly.

My cheeks flushed. 'It was my own fault. I fooled myself into thinking that I wouldn't be noticed.' Feeling undignified, I hung my head in shame.

Zak caught my serious expression. 'As if anyone could not notice you, Ellie,' he said, with a smile. 'Don't pay any attention to them; you were wonderful,' he added.

The magic of the dance still bubbling up inside me gave me the courage to meet his gaze and say, 'Thank you.'

'Will we see each other in Boston sometime?' Violet asked urgently.

'Oh yes, I hope so,' I said.

'Good. We'll keep in touch.' She handed me a slip of paper with her address on it. 'You'll write to me, let me know how you are getting on, won't you?' she said.

'Please do,' Zak said, looking earnestly at me.

'Oh, yes; yes, I will,' I promised.

Reluctantly, I left with a goodbye and a wave and swept down the iron stairs, happy to think that I might meet them both again.

As we sailed into our moorings, Alice and I took our places in a queue that was forming in steerage. The mingled smell of grease, smoke, and sea-wind from the harbour added an air of excitement among the passengers as a siren tooted. A steward shouted, 'Mind the gangplanks!' as they were opened, and swerved downwards.

The first-class passengers hastened forward. Horns honked as women in stylish coats and fluttering scarves tripped along in white high-heeled shoes, carefree beside their men. They were borne swiftly away while we waited impatiently, jammed together. Stewards leaned languidly against the railings chatting to one another, or calling out to cargo boys who were swinging huge loads on ropes, joking with each other while tipping them on to the ground.

When it was our turn, Alice and I skipped down the gangplank and, buffeted by the chill harbour winds, we thronged upon the quayside, jostling agitatedly. Finally, we were hurried through the turbulent quay and the strident noise of screeching cranes to the ferry queue for the short crossing to Ellis Island.

The ferry was crowded, but the freshness of the sea-wind enlivened us as we backed away, leaving the busy harbour, and steamed across the narrows to Ellis Island.

Six

Ellis Island looked like a whole city in itself, with its many buildings dotted around the main one. Official-looking men in uniform checked us going through. Men were separated from their women as we joined a line that led into a big hall. There we were ordered to sit down on benches in what looked like the cattle pen on our farm, and wait our turn for the doctor while official men in uniform paraded up and down, keeping an eye on us. Some of the women were frightened to go up the staircase without their husbands. Alice and I had no such fear. We had each other. Still a little off-balance, we held hands as we filed upstairs to be examined by the health inspectors.

When it came to my turn, a doctor looked me up and down then examined my eyes by rolling them backwards with a button hook. Then he examined my ears. I was passed on to another doctor who tapped my back and listened to my heartbeat. I was pronounced 'healthy' and 'fit for work', and sat waiting for Alice watching the procession of immigrants going through.

Some of the passengers had chalk marks on their shoulders: L for lungs, H for heart, L for lameness, X for signs of mental problems; X with a circle around it meant definite mental problems. E was for eyes, which was the most feared one. These people were taken to dormitories in another building.

Alice got through without a chalk mark. The health inspector insisted that we have our hair cut shorter and sent us to the YWCA cubicle. We emerged feeling like two scarecrows with our uneven mops. Red-faced and shivering with the cold, we queued at the Immigration Bureau. The officer there produced the ship's manifesto with the list of questions we were asked when boarding the ship. He looked me up and down.

'You're Eleanor O'Rourke,' he said.

'Yes.'

'What age are you?'

'Fourteen, sir.'

'Where were you born?'

'Ireland, sir.'

'Schoolgirl?'

'I'm just finished school.'

'Destination?'

'New York. I'm going to live with my uncle, Mr Jack O'Rourke, Ely Street, Brooklyn.'

'How much money do you have?'

'Five pounds.'

'Do you have an occupation waiting for you?'

'I'll be helping in my uncle's boarding house . . . and then going to college.'

Staring at our passports, he said, 'Miss Alice O'Rourke?'

Alice stepped forward. He pointed to his papers, then proceeded to ask her the same questions. There was an ominous change in the atmosphere, an extra keenness in his curious glare, as he asked if our uncle would be here to claim us. 'It's nothing personal. It's just that young girls are not safe on their own. There are people of loose morals out there, ready to take advantage of you.'

'Yes, he'll be here to meet us,' I said.

He nodded and said, 'If he ain't downstairs in the hall you'll have to go to the police station, where they can keep an eye on you until he shows up.'

Alice nudged my arm. 'Could we end up in jail if Uncle Jack doesn't show up?' she whispered.

'No, silly.'

'Will you read this please,' the official said, handing me a sheet of paper. I read it quickly, and then Alice read it. For a moment we were back in the village school, Miss Smith at her desk, stressing the importance of being able to read out loud. Finally, our papers were stamped. 'Welcome to America,' the official smiled as he handed them back to me, and giving us a fatherly smile, he waved us on.

We were directed to the left-hand side of the stairs of separation, which meant that we were free to go. The people with chalk marks went down the right-hand side of the staircase to the dormitories. Those who were directed down the centre stairs were going back to Ireland in the same ship that brought them here – but we were safely on our way.

Through the door, we found ourselves in an open hall crowded with men, women and children, and some hugging and kissing relatives they hadn't seen for a very long time. Groups of people on the far side, waiting and watchful. In the baggage hall, banks of luggage lined the walls: hat boxes on top of suitcases, trunks with portmanteaus on top of them. There was even a domed cage containing a parrot beside one suitcase. Confusion reigned as people jostled to get to the front of the queue.

'I wonder how we'll ever be able to pick Uncle Jack out of that crowd?' Alice said with dismay. 'Have you got his photograph?'

I took it out of my purse and looked at it. I noticed that it did bear a resemblance to a tall rugged man with a hard body and bunched-up shoulders standing a few feet away from us. At first glance he seemed handsome, in a smart overcoat and trilby hat, as he paced up and down, examining each passenger who passed him by. Neither of us moved as he approached. He eyed us up and down, his bushy eyebrows knitted together. 'I'm looking for Eleanor and Alice O'Rourke,' he said.

'That's us,' we said in unison.

'Are you our Uncle Jack?' Alice blurted out excitedly.

'I am,' he said brightly, turning to me. 'And you must be Ellie?'

'I am. And this is Alice.'

There was a faint stiffness in his face, which marred the lustre of his blue eyes and the strength of his handshake. He shifted uncomfortably. 'You managed to get here in one piece then?'

'Yes.'

'Good,' he smiled warmly at last.

'Well, come on. Follow me.' He stooped down, lifted our case and walked rapidly ahead of us. We left to a murmur of farewells from the friends we'd made on our voyage, and followed Uncle Jack as he tramped over the gangway on to a waiting ferry.

As we walked, he asked after Mam and Aunt Mabel. Mam's health seemed the main thing that concerned him. Talking of her brought me a pang of loneliness, but Uncle Jack seemed kind and his protective air seemed to promise that he would take care of us. He would open up a whole new world to us, full of wonderful possibilities.

We alighted at a quay named Castle Clinton and followed him over gangway slats on to the pavement. Once outside he glanced up and down, then he took off up a narrow lane. We hurried after him, climbing a steep path as he went on ahead out on to a street full of cars and vans. After all the speculation and doubt and the long journey, we were here, walking along a New York street.

Uncle Jack took a right turn to where there were shops and people and cafés. The hot, pungent smell of roasting coffee beans and baking bread made my stomach feel hollow with hunger. Uncle Jack dodged nimbly through the traffic, his tall figure bouncing along, hardly bothering to check that we were still behind him. Easy enough for him, I thought, he was used to the traffic. We did our best to keep up with him but the jostling crowd and the lack of sleep meant that we fell back. I wanted to shout 'Wait for us!' but it didn't seem the thing to do.

'Here we are,' he said, lifting the rear door of a van and piling our cases into the back.

Alice was reluctant to get into the van and gripped the door in fear. I pushed her in and jumped in after her. Uncle Jack got into the front seat. He turned on the engine. It burst into life, hissing and spitting, startling us. 'Now off we go,' he said, easing out into the traffic.

'We're going to die,' Alice cried plaintively, cowering sideways into her corner as we shuddered forward.

'Don't be silly,' Uncle Jack laughed, and, shoulders stiff, he steadied the big wheel in front of him and manoeuvred his way through the traffic, us gripping our seats tightly.

'Not so bad, now is it?' he said, neck red from the exertion.

'No,' Alice said reluctantly, glad of the safety of the back seat.

Cars speeded past us going in the opposite direction. In the middle of the road, streetcars as big as buses clanged along. 'Trolley-cars,' Uncle Jack said.

We drove along by the dock piers of the river, past blocks of dull shops and apartments, a factory here and there among demolition lots. To our right the Hudson River glittered; ocean-going ships sailed out beyond the cranes. Close up, the skyscrapers were sharp-edged and dark, like huge faceless giants.

'Manhattan,' said Uncle Jack. As I looked up at the buildings towering above me, I felt a strong surge of excitement.

We crossed a bridge. The sunlight through the girders flickered on the black river, where the red, white and blue flags of ferries stretched out taut in the wind. 'Brooklyn Bridge,' he said, stretching himself over the wheel, pointing out the famous landmark with a sharp movement of his hand.

Awestruck, Alice leaned forward and asked, 'Do you love it here, Uncle Jack?'

'I have to like it, I don't have a choice. Back in Ireland I couldn't make a living. Here, our boarding house pays its way. Each year we do a little better.'

We drove along a cobbled street lined with faded

buildings, then lurched downhill, on to shop-lined streets. 'Out here are the neighbourhoods, with their separate communities,' Uncle Jack explained as we passed whole sections of the old, dingy part of the city going off in all directions – some buildings were even barricaded up with corrugated fronts. Nervous, Alice sank further down into her seat.

When we reached what Uncle Jack called 'the suburbs' there were endless streets that sprawled out, broken occasionally by shops here and there. The buildings grew more shabby and down-at-heel. He drove on in silence past tall, disorderly houses set back from the road. He stopped outside one such gangling house. It was painted brown and had elaborate carved decorations around the eaves.

'Here we are,' he said, parking his van in a narrow space outside it.

I got out of the van and looked at the house. How many times had I read the address on the envelopes? Never in my wildest dreams did I imagine that one day I'd be standing outside it. I caught the eye of a woman looking down at us from out of an upstairs window, and waved, thinking that it must be Aunt Sally. She didn't wave back.

Uncle Jack carried our cases up the steps and through a porch to a big brown front door that he opened with a key. Then he released a chain and ushered us into a hallway. It smelt of polish and damp; the wallpaper was brown with blue patterned flowers. There was a hallstand full of coats and umbrellas, a telephone on it.

Excited, but a little apprehensive, we followed Uncle Jack down a narrow stairwell covered with brown linoleum to a ground-floor kitchen that looked out on a back yard. A woman in a flowered-print overall over a black dress was standing at a range, cooking. She wasn't young, but she had a soft kind face, framed with dark feathery hair.

'Hello Aunt Sally,' Alice said brightly, going to her, extending her hand politely.

'I'm Bridget,' the woman said, but with a hint of a smile. 'Your aunt is resting. Go quiet and easy now, she's not too lively today,' she said.

The kitchen was homely. There was a huge range, and along one wall were cupboards filled with china, glasses of various shapes and plates, cups and saucers and bowls. Bridget told us to sit down, asking if we were hungry. We were ravenous. She served us a plateful of eggs and beans each.

As we were finishing our meal, a thin girl of about Alice's age bounded into the kitchen, her pigtails bobbing. 'I'm Mary-Pat,' she said, perching herself on a chair opposite us, drawing her knees up to her chin, to stare sullenly at us through big, dark eyes. 'I'm your cousin,' she added coyly. 'Mom says she'll see you later on. What're your names?' she asked.

'I'm Ellie.'

'And I'm Alice,' Alice said through a mouthful of food.

Eventually, Aunt Sally came downstairs. A tall, stylish woman in a black dress, though she must have been beautiful once, her dark hair was arranged in a kind of severe helmet around her strained face. She extended a ringed hand to shake mine. 'How do you do?' she said formally, looking me up and down without expression. 'How was your voyage?' Her voice was coldly sweet as, without waiting for a reply, she went on, 'I do hate all those crowds, and of course I knew that your uncle couldn't wait to meet his little nieces all by himself.' She lit a cigarette, shook out the match. 'Now, I'll show you to your rooms,' she said, businesslike.

We followed her up two flights of stairs, along a corridor, past closed doors and a bathroom, and up a very narrow flight of stairs to a small bedroom at the top of the house. 'Here we are,' she announced, looking about her with satisfaction.

It was cramped. There were two iron beds, a cupboard, and an oilcloth-covered table with a basin on it. The view from the sash window was of the scarred brick walls of tenement buildings and fire escapes.

'It's very high up,' Alice said, almost afraid to look down.

'It'll do for you,' Aunt Sally said tersely, adding, 'and you won't be spending much time here as it is.' Seeing the look on our faces, she went on, 'You will be needed

82

downstairs. It's difficult running a boarding house these days.' She clasped her hands together and moved back to the door. 'Now, I think I'll go and have my bath while you unpack.'

'Thank you, Aunt Sally,' we said in unison, watching as she closed the door behind her and went to deal with things that were obviously more important than we were.

A water tank gurgled above us. We looked at one another uncertainly. Alice burst into tears. 'I want to go home,' she cried.

I put my arms around her. 'Hush, don't cry, you'll be all right. You have me to look after you.' I stroked her hair reassuringly, though thoughts of Mam swirled around in my head. I imagined her sitting at the kitchen table, her face screwed up as she tried to calculate if she could afford all the extra things she would need for the new baby. I felt an awful wave of longing for her and for home.

While Alice lay on her bed, sniffing, I unpacked our things, which took up very little space in the wardrobe. I told Alice to wash her face and hands in the small sink in our room, as I did after her. We changed into cleaner dresses before plucking up the courage to go downstairs.

We found Aunt Sally in what I guessed was the parlour. She didn't raise her eyes from the blooms she was fiddling with, but when she had finished she turned to us, noting with grudging approval our clean clothes.

'Let me show you the dining room,' she said, leading the way into a room and standing back with her arms folded, waiting for us to be impressed.

It was a large, oppressive room. Along one wall there was a huge sideboard on which stood containers, serving implements, and folded table napkins. In the middle of the room there was a long table, rows of chairs lined up on either side of it. 'This is where you'll be spending a lot of your time,' she said, walking around the table.

I stood silently, wondering how long it took to clean it up after a meal.

'And this is the living room for our lodgers,' she said, leading the way into the next room. There was a huge fireplace with a velour sofa on either side of it, a low table in the centre, and several upholstered armchairs in brown velvet. At one end was a piano next to a big window, through which I looked at the buildings and beyond them at the Brooklyn Bridge, which looked from this distance as though it were made from mesh and lace. I was wondering what lay on the far side of it when Aunt Sally's voice cut into my thoughts. 'You're not paying attention, Eleanor.'

'Sorry, I was wondering what's it's like on the other side of that bridge.'

She followed my gaze as if seeing the bridge for the first time. 'Out there are separate communities,' she said. 'There are all different nationalities in the different neighbourhoods: Spanish, Armenians, Russians, and

Italians are around Mulberry Street between the Chinese and the Jewish quarter. The Germans are on the Upper East Side. We prefer to keep ourselves to ourselves here.' She looked at me sternly. 'You won't be crossing that bridge. Not on your own.'

'Is this the Irish quarter?' Alice asked.

'The Irish are scattered all over,' Aunt Sally said, dismissively. 'They work as policemen, railroad men, bartenders, and drivers of Central Park horse-cabs.' Suddenly her face brightened as she added proudly, 'Our St Patrick's Day parade is the biggest parade of all.'

Over a dinner of Irish stew cooked by Bridget, in the family room, Aunt Sally complained that it was impossible to find help. She talked about her doctor, and said that he was the only person who realised how ill she'd been. 'He's been marvellous,' she said. 'I shouldn't be here without him. Isn't that right, Jack?'

Uncle Jack only grunted in response.

Mary-Pat seemed to have taken to Alice though. She talked to her in a low voice about her school, leaving me out of the conversation.

A tall, slender boy came into the room. He was taller than Aunt Sally, nearly as tall as Uncle Jack was, with wider eyes and thicker hair. He swaggered over to his seat, looking over at Alice and I, with the assurance of someone who is aware of his good looks. Seating himself opposite me, he stared in my direction.

'This is my son – your cousin – Eamon,' said Aunt Sally, looking fondly at him. 'Eamon, this is Eleanor and Alice.'

Eamon nodded. 'How do you do – Eleanor, Alice,' he replied smoothly, taking his napkin out of its holder. 'Irish stew!' he said enthusiastically. 'Delicious! I could eat a horse!' Aunt Sally beamed, Uncle Jack frowned a little, and Alice giggled.

As he ate, Eamon kept catching my eye, and I would look away quickly, embarrassed to have been noticed.

Later, in our bedroom, I went to the window to pull down the old blind. After we'd said our prayers, Alice and I crawled into our freezing cold beds with lumpy mattresses.

The room was eerily quiet at first. I closed my eyes, opened them, and closed them again. Shivering, I began to hear the strange sounds of the house: Bridget washing dishes, Aunt Sally laughing with someone, then a succession of goodnights, and moans and groans, and finally snoring. The room seemed to float in darkness. I could taste my tears on my lips as I closed my eyes, wondering if I could hold them back for Alice's sake.

'Ellie, I can't sleep.' Alice's voice was plaintive.

I got into her bed. We snuggled up together, warming one another. When I heard the steady sound of her breathing I went back to my own bed and tossed and turned, trying to find a warm spot in the lumpy mattress. I thought of the garden and fields of Ireland, the sea and the birds. I thought of Mam missing her own home, the spirit gone out of her, and longed to be with her.

Nothing in Aunt Mabel's books and photographs had prepared me for New York, with its contrasts of beauty and poverty. Nothing had prepared me for unfriendly, evasive Aunt Sally, either.

Seven

Alarm clocks reverberated around the house waking me with a start, then, realising where I was, I lay back on the pillows and fell asleep again.

A loud banging on our door woke me out of a deep sleep. I threw back the covers and jumped out of bed just as Aunt Sally came into the room. Dressed up in a black suit, her sly eyes shaded by the brim of a hat with a peacock feather in it, she looked like one of those faded film stars I'd seen in Aunt Mabel's magazines.

'I didn't expect you to sleep late. It is half past eight already,' she said.

'I'm sorry, we didn't realise the time,' I said, jumping out of bed.

Aunt Sally ignored this. 'I'm going out. When I come back I expect you both to be up, dressed and downstairs attending to your duties.' She left, banging the door behind her.

'I can't wake up.' Alice groaned, lifted her head, and gradually pushed herself up on her elbows. 'I'll stay in bed for a while. You go.' She collapsed back in bed and fell fast asleep.

A frail light seeped through the curtains. I ran down to the bathroom in my bare feet, my coat over my nightdress, splashed my face and hands with soapy water and brushed my teeth.

Alice was still asleep when I got back. 'Come on, you have to get up.' I shook her. She got slowly out of bed and stumbled to the bathroom.

I dressed, brushed my hair, and pulled the blinds. Bright sunshine flooded the bedroom, giving us needed warmth. When Alice returned, we made our beds and opened the window. Along the passage there was the sound of people rising, doors banging, water running. We made our way down to the kitchen, where Bridget poured us a cup of coffee and gave us each a slice of buttered toast. 'That's to wake you up,' she said, handing me my coffee. The first sip made me cough. She gave us an apron each from a peg on the back of the door. 'Breakfast is nearly over, the dining room needs clearing up,' she said wearily.

'But I haven't finished,' Alice said, sipping her coffee, before catching Bridget's raised eyebrow. She put down her cup and hastily followed me to the dining room.

The lodgers greeted us with curious good mornings. They were tough-looking men, with lean set faces and broad square shoulders. Cramped together, heads down, they were busy polishing off the food on their plates. One by one they left as we cleared up, taking with them the wrapped sandwiches that Bridget had made for them. One man whistled as he passed me. I kept my eyes down.

After they had all left, Bridget washed the dishes. Alice and I dried them. As soon as the last plate was put away she handed me a mop and bucket and told me to wash the kitchen floor. I swished the mop in circles, rinsed it out, longing to collapse back into bed. But then I was told to mop the passageway.

'Now the upstairs,' Bridget said, 'And bring down the dirty laundry.' She handed Alice polish, Vim and cloths.

I squeezed out the mop, got a fresh bucket of water and Alice and I climbed the stairs to the first floor where we began cleaning the dim, unfamiliar rooms at the back of the house. I pulled curtains in the first one to let the light stream in, and opened the window to get rid of the stale smell of sleep. It overlooked an asphalt yard with a clothesline, and a shed, and a bare patch of grass, and fire escape to the left. There were no trees to climb, or places to hide.

We spent the rest of the morning cleaning each bedroom. I vacuumed, while Alice dusted and tidied up each room. In the two bathrooms we picked up the dirty towels, put them in the laundry baskets, cleaned the showers, hand basins, toilets, and mopped the floors.

Behind one of the doors we heard snoring, so we didn't go in. When the last of the rooms were done, we sat down on one of the beds to have a rest.

'I don't like it here.' Alice's voice shook.

'It'll be all right. This is only temporary. Soon you'll be off to school, and I'll be going to college,' I said, putting my arm around her.

We took the laundry down for Bridget to put in a huge washing machine. 'I'm hungry,' Alice told Bridget.

She sat us down at the kitchen table and gave us each a mug of coffee and a sandwich of delicious cold ham from an 'ice-box'. We ate ravenously, huddled at the end of the table.

Aunt Sally returned. She seemed a bit more light-hearted and there was a glow in her cheeks.

'How're they doing?' she asked Bridget.

'Fine,' Bridget replied, keeping her back to Aunt Sally, while rinsing out the dishcloths. 'They're not afraid of hard work.'

'That's one good thing about them,' Aunt Sally said, as though we weren't in the room, helping herself to a cup of coffee. Then she turned to me. 'Hurry up and get back to your chores. I expect all the rooms to be done by lunchtime.'

Bridget rattled her pots and pans. 'Give them a chance to settle in. They're only children,' she said.

Aunt Sally stared into her coffee cup, a furrow etched

on her brow. 'Everyone in this house has to earn his or her keep,' she said crisply.

Bridget didn't say much more in front of Aunt Sally, but when she left and we heard the slam of the hall door, she said, 'This is no place for young girls like the two of you. This is a boarding house for workmen, and some of them are rough. It's not right.'

After lunch she told Alice and I to go and have a quick nap. '. . . While her ladyship is out,' she said with a wink.

Bridget did all of the cooking. Each morning, in her black dress buttoned up to the throat and her flowery overall, she padded silently around the kitchen preparing breakfast with the dedication of a priest saying Mass. The men left at seven o'clock and didn't return until suppertime. At first we felt embarrassed around them. They could be coarse and they seemed to swear a lot; but they were nice, Irish men who had come to New York for work and found jobs mostly at the docks. They came back exhausted every evening to a dinner of bacon or Irish stew. We were given the leftovers when the wash up was done.

There were three flights of stairs, twelve stairs in each one, not counting the steps to the kitchen. Each day I counted them as I cleaned them down. All of the ten bedrooms were occupied.

Aunt Sally kept a close eye on us. Even in a house that

big there was no escaping her. She would appear out of nowhere and drag her index finger along a mantelpiece or a chest of drawers, while we looked on awaiting her verdict.

When I asked her if we could go out for a walk one afternoon, she wagged her finger disapprovingly at me, saying, 'There is no going out while there's work to be done.'

'We're not servants,' Alice said brazenly.

Aunt Sally looked angrily at her. 'You are not here for a holiday either. Do you understand?'

'Yes, Aunt,' she said meekly.

Aunt Sally stood in front of the dressing-table mirror, tidying her hair. 'You're both lucky you're not being sent out to train as parlour maids or waitresses in some strange dingy hotel.'

Alice put her thumb in her mouth. I said, 'We're here to better ourselves.'

She turned to me. I met her gaze. 'Yes, well, meantime, there's no harm in learning a few basic domestic chores.'

I wrote home telling Mam about the skyscrapers, the noise of the traffic going so fast, and all the different nationalities living close by. I described the house and the view from Brooklyn Bridge. *Aunt Sally is in charge. Uncle Jack doesn't say much. He leaves for work early and doesn't get home until late. It is so different from home. The hours are long; we're exhausted by the time we get to bed.'*

I didn't want to complain too much, so I crossed out the last two sentences and described the food instead. When I finished it, I looked out of the window over the roofs. The rain was coming down in a steady torrent, flowing out of the gullies, taking with it twigs and bits of debris. It reminded me of the rain at home. How when the river burst its banks it drowned the lower field, leaving the whole place awash. Thinking of home filled me with a longing for those fields, the sea-breeze on my face, and the thatched-roofed cottages along the sea-road. I turned from the window and lay back on my bed, my eyes fixed on the sloping ceiling, and cried.

Eight

Alice and I soon fell into a routine. Each morning we ate our toast in tiny bites between serving the tables, while Bridget padded to and fro absently humming as she cooked. Then we started on the bedrooms, our arms aching, our shoulders painful from the previous day's work. We pulled back the heavy old drapes in each room and made the bed, polished the enormous dark furniture, dusted the bookshelves and cupboards.

Once, from one of the bedrooms, I heard Aunt Sally and Uncle Jack arguing, their voices rising and falling. I didn't hear what they were saying, only the sound of their voices: hers raised in accusation, his high and defensive. He stormed out past me, not noticing that I was there.

Up until then I had no idea of their relationship towards one another, and had been only concerned with their attitude towards Alice and me. Now, I noticed an unpleasantness that made them seem unhappy with one another.

Aunt Sally came out of her bedroom. 'Go and clean the family room,' she ordered me crossly, without looking me in the eye. I wondered what had made them both so angry, and why Uncle Jack hadn't gone to work.

Eamon was in the family room, drinking coffee and smoking a cigarette.

'Well, how's Miss Irish?'

'Well, thank you.'

'So, do you like it here?'

'It's a very big house, a lot of rooms to clean.'

'I suppose it seems so after living in a cottage,' he smirked. 'This is a three-generation house. My great-grandfather bought it. He started out as a labourer on the docks. He did all sorts of jobs to get the money together to buy this place, I can tell you. But he made it. He was a revered public figure in this part of the city before he passed away, leaving it all to Mom. It can be depressing at times,' he went on, looking around the room. 'I'm OK because I'm pretty well left alone, and I have my books.'

'I love books too.'

'You probably like romantic novels, with dark brooding knights in shining armour and innocent girls full of great sorrow and joy,' he said, mocking me.

'I like all kinds of books,' I said stiffly.

Ignoring that remark, he said, 'Well, you're lucky to be here; I hope you appreciate it.'

'Oh, I do,' I lied.

As I polished every surface and carefully dusted each one of the china ornaments, his eyes were fixed on my every move, but when I caught his eye he shifted his gaze to the window. I was about to leave when he rattled his cup on its saucer. 'You can bring me another cup of coffee on your way back.'

'I'm not going to the kitchen,' I said, walking out the door.

'You are now,' he said coldly.

In the kitchen, my hand trembled with anger as I poured coffee into his cup. So what if his grandfather was someone important and he was the son and heir to this house! There was no need for him to treat me like a servant.

'Forget it,' he said when I returned and handed it to him. 'I've changed my mind. I'm going out.'

I was glad to see him go. As soon as I heard the hall door slam, I opened the window to get rid of the stale smell of smoke.

'Eamon's rude,' I said to Bridget afterwards.

'His mother spoils him,' Bridget said. 'But keep out of his way. As soon as he gets his holidays he'll be out all day. He's got a job doing deliveries for the firm of Builders' Provider your Uncle Jack works for.'

I went back upstairs, where Alice and I stripped the bed in Aunt Sally and Uncle Jack's room and put fresh sheets on it. Alice removed all the cosmetics from the glass-topped dressing table, wiped all the fancy jars and bottles with a damp cloth, and lined them up neatly together: cold cream, night cream.

'I wonder if we'll ever own stylish things like this?' she said, wistfully gazing into Aunt Sally's wardrobe.

'We'll have far nicer things, and we'll live in a mansion in Manhattan. We'll have our very own automobile, and I'll learn to drive it.'

'Oh Ellie, do you really think we will?'

'I know it,' I assured her.

Eamon's bedroom was up in the loft. It was simply furnished with an old couch that had been mended here and there. The shelves were filled with books, rows and rows of them in covers of pale gold and shiny red. Some of them were battered old books; all of them were invitingly interesting. There was a book of Shakespeare plays and an anthology of English poets. I took down *The Raven* by Edgar Allen Poe, opened and began reading it. It scared me. I thought of school and Miss Smith, who would have read it to us in an understanding way.

I put down my duster and polish and looked down through the small window out on to the street. All the houses looked the same: identical brown brick with cheap varnished front doors, fanlights overhead, and similar front gardens. Most of them were apartments, every available space rented out. Aunt Sally had inherited this suffocating house from her father, crammed with its awful furniture, dull carpets and curtains, just as they'd left it. The lodgers were doubtless inherited, too.

I despaired that I could ever feel at home here, and knew that if ever I was to feel at home anywhere I'd have to make something of myself first. What I wouldn't have given that minute to see the fields and hedgerows of home, spread out like a patchwork quilt. And the village, where the old men sat talking in the square, and everyone would say hello to you.

Dusk was drawing down, light leaked from the landing. I went to look for Alice in our bedroom to wash up for serving dinner. Alice was sitting on her bed, darning socks.

'I hate Aunt Sally, she's horrible and bossy,' she said, almost in tears. I couldn't think of anything to say to comfort and reassure her. 'And she drinks gin cocktails by herself,' she added.

'Shh . . . don't say that,' I said. 'You'll get into trouble if anyone hears you.'

'I don't care if she does hear me,' she said, defiantly.

But despite Alice's feelings, she and Mary-Pat were becoming very friendly. They played together in the evenings, a game of 'Hollywood' in which they were film stars, arrayed in old ballgowns of Aunt Sally's and her glittering fake jewellery. Mary-Pat always played the star role. Alice had become addicted to these games, and was such a good companion to Mary-Pat that Aunt Sally started to soften towards her. She said Alice was a talented, pretty girl and she was glad Mary-Pat had made a friend of her. It wasn't long before Alice was let off most of her duties around the house, which left me to carry out the housework.

One day, Aunt Sally announced that she was sending Alice to the St Joseph's Academy with Mary-Pat, and that she wouldn't be expected to help around the house any more.

'When do I apply for college?' I couldn't help asking. If Alice was to be educated then why couldn't I be? But my question was met with stony-faced silence and I knew I would be cleaning rooms all day, every day. Uncle Jack had promised Mam to send us both to school. Had he forgotten?

'That's not possible, Ellie,' he said, awkwardly, when I found time to talk to him. He looked guiltily at me under his craggy brows.

'But I came here to get myself an education, Uncle Jack,' I protested.

He studied the carpet. 'Your aunt needs the help at the moment; she hasn't been well.'

I stalked out of the room full of indignation. Help was when someone gave you a hand with the workload. Aunt Sally didn't do a tap.

On the morning Alice started school, Aunt Sally made her parade up and down the kitchen. In her brand-new blue blazer with a gold crest that was far too big for her, and a white blouse and pleated skirt, she looked so grown-up. Her hair had been washed in Aunt Sally's scented shampoo and was braided neatly behind her ears. I bit my tongue to stop myself from begging to be allowed to go too and gave her my special Child of Mary medal to keep her safe and told her to pay attention to the teachers and learn all she could.

'I'll learn everything,' she said, skipping out the door without a backward glance. Mary-Pat turned at the gate and gave me a malicious grin as I waved them goodbye.

I spent that day going from room to room, keeping out of everyone's way. Cleaning on my own was lonely and boring. I missed Alice. When she came home that evening with a gold star on her exercise book, puffed out with tales of cheerful girls escorting her round the playground and nice teachers encouraging her, I was delighted for her, but heartbroken too. I wanted to be writing exercises and talking of exciting subjects with classmates.

With Aunt Sally I fared worse than ever. Whatever I was doing she'd swoop down on me, hawk-like, with her sharp, tight-lipped criticism. She picked on the smallest faults she could find with me. 'You're daydreaming as usual,' she'd say, or 'You're not doing a proper job.' There was no pleasing her. I would have to bite my tongue to keep myself from answering her back. She would notice my resentment and say, 'Who's to tell you these things if I don't?'

When Alice was upset because she'd been in trouble in class, Aunt Sally would blame the teachers. The more I grew to loathe my aunt, it seemed Alice grew to be her ally. 'She's good to me, Ellie,' she said, when we were alone.

'It's all right for you, you have her on your side now, you can do no wrong,' I said sourly. I could never do anything right. Worse than that, I was despised, left out of everything that went on in the house. If I was to have any kind of future I would have to bide my time and study on my own. I would borrow one or two of Eamon's books to start with. I would set our alarm clock and get up at five o'clock in the morning, when the house was quiet and read them.

One morning, when I thought everyone was out, I went into Eamon's room and shut the door. I was choosing a book to borrow when I heard the tread of footsteps on the corridor. Nervously, I watched the light fall across the room as his long, thin neck appeared aggressively round the door. I jumped up from the bed and retreated into the shadows, fear welling up inside me.

'So,' he said, standing before me, his eyes hot with contempt. 'What are you doing with that?'

My heart leaped into my throat. 'I was just looking . . . I'm sorry.'

'You were snooping,' he hissed as he came towards me, his sleeves rolled up, his chest heaving. He wrenched the book from my hand. It fell to the floor. 'Pick it up.' His face as red as a brick, he went on, 'Who do you think you are, walking in here whenever you like, without a by your leave, and rummaging through my things?' His bony hands glided gently over the book. 'These are *my* books. I never allow anyone to put a finger on them.'

'I'm sorry, I only wanted to —'

'Stop saying "sorry",' he barked. 'I could get you into serious trouble for this. Mother will think you have nothing better to do.' He edged over to me, put his arm round my waist. 'But I won't tell if you don't.' His eyes bore into me; his heavy wet lips sought mine.

I caught my breath, edged back. 'Don't touch me,' I said.

'What's the matter? You got someone else?'

'No.'

'What, then?'

'I don't like you.'

'You'll change your mind.'

I had this terrible urge to laugh into his face. Instead I pushed him with sudden force and sent him reeling backwards.

I flew from the room but he followed me the length of the passage. 'You've been avoiding me,' he said, in a whisper behind me.

'So?'

'It bothers me.'

I went to walk past him. He blocked my way. 'I think you and I should have a little talk, don't you?'

'About what?'

He reached out and grabbed my shoulders. 'About the fact that you're not being very respectful towards me,' he said.

'I have nothing to say to you.'

'Why?' His eyes widened in mock surprise.

'Because . . . I just haven't.' I kept my face averted.

'You're resentful of the fact that I'm going to college and you're not,' he taunted.

'Maybe. I didn't come here to be a slave to you and your family.' Tears stung my eyes but I blinked them back.

'You have to pay your way and Alice's.' His voice was cold and superior.

'Well, I don't intend being a servant here for much longer.'

He gave a short rasping laugh. 'You don't have a choice. Where else can you go?'

Nine

Aunt Sally, with her airs and graces, decided to hold afternoon tea parties. As if I wasn't busy enough she turned me into a 'proper maid'. She bought me a maid's outfit: a black dress and a white frilly apron. She taught me how to walk more gracefully, with my head held high, how to carry a tea tray elegantly, and speak to her friends in a genteel manner. Reclining in her armchair, smiling smugly, she would check my nails for cleanliness and make sure that the white collar of my dress and my apron were snow-white. I would serve tiny sandwiches with the crusts cut off and dainty iced cakes to her friends. Aunt Sally would sit upright; her hair swept back, her make-up perfect, chatting away.

One day, I went out to the yard to hang up the washing. Alice and Mary-Pat were there, sitting side by side on the swing. Dressed in Aunt Sally's high heels and her old clothes, their legs crossed primly, pretending to smoke, they were playing one of their favourite games, 'Ladies'. Their voices rose and fell in an affected manner as they spoke to one another. They stopped when they saw me.

'Aren't you too hot dressed up like that?' I smiled.

'No, silly.' Alice heaved a sigh and with a toss of a big old handbag indicated her impatience with me.

They glanced at one another in a secretive way, and then Mary-Pat stared at me, waiting for me to go. I was an intruder. As I turned away I could hear them giggling, but I was too heavy-hearted, too miserable to be annoyed with Alice. Tired of the smell of old carpets and dust, polish and disinfectant, I'd been hoping for a bit of company.

The kitchen smelled of hot clothes. Bridget was standing lopsided over the ironing board, ironing the heavy linen sheets. She looked tired and dishevelled. There were red spots on her cheeks, and her legs in her thick stockings were swollen.

'I can finish off this lot,' I said, feeling sorry for her.

She looked at me with gratitude. 'Thanks. I'll make us a fresh pot of coffee first.'

'You're very quiet,' she said, when I took a break. 'Is anything wrong?'

I sipped my coffee, my feet hooked around the rung of a chair. 'Alice hasn't any time for me any more, and Eamon seems to get a kick out of humiliating me, and Uncle Jack doesn't ever stick up for me.' Feeling sorry for myself now, I swallowed the lump in my throat.

She leaned towards me. 'Don't take any notice of

Alice. She's just a child enjoying a new friendship. Eamon'll soon be off to college and you'll be left in peace,' she said in a low voice.

I sighed. 'Lucky Eamon.' I bit my lip, wondering if I'd gone too far.

'As for your Uncle Jack. It's not his fault. The poor man is not the master of his own home. She never lets him forget that it's her house. He's under her thumb. I wouldn't mind, but he's so good to her, giving her everything she wants – but she's a mean-spirited woman.'

'How do you stick it here, Bridget?' I asked, helping myself to more coffee.

She shrugged. 'I keep out of it. My function is to cook meals. Granted, it's not much of a life here, but I stay for your uncle. He wouldn't get a proper meal otherwise. I feel sorry for him.' Her face went red with embarrassment, as if she'd revealed too much and regretted it. I had a sudden realisation that she was in love with my uncle. The words were hardly out of her mouth though when we heard Aunt Sally's footstep in the hall. I leaped into a flurry of activity, running the iron smoothly over a sheet.

'How did the doctor find you?' Bridget asked her.

Aunt Sally lifted her fur-covered shoulders. 'Much better, though naturally I'm not a well woman. But the visits do cheer me up. He's such a good doctor, one in a million.' She made a puffing noise, as though she was drawing her last breath. 'Shouldn't you be doing the rooms?' she asked me briskly.

'She's giving me a hand.' Bridget winked at me behind her back.

When she left, Bridget leaned forward, tucked a stray strand of hair behind my ear. 'You mustn't let her get you down,' she said.

I felt comforted. I thought how different Bridget was from Aunt Sally. She didn't look down on me or despise me. She treated me like a human being – as well as keeping a maternal eye on me. As I ironed, she told me about her family. She hailed from County Cork also. The eldest of ten children, she'd come to America with one of her brothers, to find work to help support them. Her brother, a friend of Uncle Jack's, had introduced her to him and, liking her on sight, Uncle Jack had employed her. I was a good audience for her nostalgic stories because, in that awful house, I was an outsider.

One day, Aunt Sally announced that she was going to visit her sister in San Francisco. She flung herself into shopping for her trip so I didn't see much of her for days. The morning she was leaving, she came downstairs dressed in a sombre coat and a black felt hat with a short veil over her face. She looked like a widow in mourning on her way to a funeral. Through her veil she told me in an affected voice, 'Do what Bridget tells you, Ellie, and try to be cheerful to the lodgers.'

'You can make yourself useful,' Bridget said cheerfully, when Aunt Sally had left. 'I need a few things from the store.' She gave me a list, money in a purse, and directions to the 'village'.

I was relieved to get out of the house. Light-heartedly, I stepped out into the early morning. The street was wet, puddles everywhere. Rainwater dripped from every nook and crevice of the dull buildings that seemed to engulf me. I walked along, trying to get a feel for the place and memorise each block. Further on, the skyscrapers had a threatening quality. I stopped outside each store and pressed my face to the window, acknowledging the difference of this place. The air smelled of herbs and spices. I did my shopping, then moved from window to window, looking at everything. I kept walking along, pausing outside a pub to sniff the familiar smell of beer that made me homesick. People surged past. Shrill voices rang out. Strange-looking men cast crude glances at me as I passed by, jarring my nerves. It was a new experience, better than the mindless routine of making beds and cleaning floors. Would I ever come to grips with it?

I was standing under a store awning, sheltering from the rain, when a van pulled up with an unnecessary screech of brakes. I turned to see Eamon at the wheel. I watched, downcast, as he parked in front of me.

'Want a lift?' he said.

I moved out and started walking.

'No sense in getting wet,' he called out. 'C'mon . . . Hop in.'

I couldn't think of an excuse not to and, reluctant to incur any more hostility from my cousin, I turned back to the van and slid into the passenger seat. He pulled out into the traffic, accelerated and took off. I gripped the seat; pressed myself back into it, trying to be invisible.

'So, what're you doin' out all by yourself?' he asked, taking his eyes off the road to look at me.

'Bridget sent me on some errands,' I said.

He blared out the horn as he approached an intersection, almost frightening a horse to death, then speeded towards the end of the block. When we finally arrived at our street, I was practically clawing at the door handle.

'Thanks,' I said, jumping out as soon as we got to the house.

As the van door slammed behind me I was sure I heard him laugh, but I settled inside as quickly as I could.

That evening, he watched me as I cleared the plates and cutlery and washed and dried them, as if something about the way I worked could tell him more about me.

Bridget, observing this, said to me after he'd gone, 'I think you should have an early night. At least you can be alone in your room, have a little privacy.'

I twisted round to take a closer look at her. Her eyes

were sad; the skin of her neck was rough. She looked tired and old, I thought. We were quiet for a moment before she said, 'I left home when I was a bit older than you were, but I went to work for strangers. Strangers are better, if you ask me.' Her tone implied that this was something I was beginning to discover for myself.

'I thought Aunt Sally would be kinder,' I said wearily.

Bridget handed me a bunch of grapes she'd hidden for me, and closed the door. 'She wasn't always severe. They used to give parties and laugh a lot.' She spoke with a sadness that startled me. 'Oh, they were lovely times. There was champagne and marvellous food at Christmas time. I couldn't enjoy them at first, I was so scared of making a fool of myself, but your Uncle Jack was so kind. He talked to me when I was lonely.' She looked into the distance. 'After little Amy died, your Aunt Sally became very ill and your poor uncle retreated into himself.' She continued mixing and stirring, absorbed in her tale.

'Amy? Who's Amy?'

Bridget looked at me, frowning, as if wondering why I didn't know. 'The baby. She was so beautiful. Always clapping her hands to be lifted out of her cot. I used to bath her every evening. Oh, the things we suffer in this life! Your uncle tried his best with your aunt after the little one died, but she was inconsolable for months – years – and he eventually lost patience with her. She was a mess; just dragged around the house, her heart broken.'

I sat, shocked at what Bridget had just told me. It certainly explained a lot about Aunt Sally's behaviour. But why had no one told me, or our family, about little Amy? And why was her name never mentioned in this house?

As I dusted, swept, and ironed, I thought about baby Amy and felt a little more sympathetic towards my aunt, knowing what I did. I didn't like her any more than I ever had, but I learned to let her barbed remarks float over my head.

And I was growing to like the lodgers. One of them, Jim, was an Irish Republican. He was sending money home for 'the cause,' he told me. He often got into arguments with the other lodgers, who said he was deluded. I longed to tell him about Ed and his escapades, but Bridget warned me against it.

Meanwhile, Alice was going to Irish dancing classes with Mary-Pat. Decked out in Irish costumes, hair beribboned, ringlets bouncing, they were happy together as they danced round one another in little circles to the admiration and approval of Uncle Jack and Aunt Sally. Mary-Pat fluttered about the house – a bright, pretty girl, and not the sourpuss she once was. There was no more flouncing off in terrible rages. Aunt Sally was delighted with her.

If Bridget hadn't insisted that I buy fresh fish on Fridays I might never have had any time off. When Friday came, I could escape for a few hours. My heart would quicken as I left the house. I loved watching people of all nationalities going by: women in their long coloured robes and turbans, dark-suited men hurrying somewhere important as if they didn't have a minute to spare. So different from home, where time was what we had most of. I would stroll along, thinking how distant home seemed; the golden trailing ribbons of gorse through the fields, and the honeysuckle reddening on the hedgerows, the cool green moss by the riverbank, and pink-beige sand and blue sea.

By the end of the first month, I began to feel certain that there was no prospect of any other kind of life for me but the one I had, unless luck came my way. Also, I was growing out of my clothes, and so was Alice. 'I'll have to buy some material and make us some summer clothes,' I said to her.

Alice swung her silky head. 'I'd like a pink frock like Mary-Pat's good one.'

I smiled. 'I'll make you one,' I said, thinking how much she was blossoming into a graceful young girl.

'I feel bad about Mam and Lucy,' Alice said. 'I'm afraid I'll forget them.'

'Of course you won't. Anyway, you'll go back to visit them one day.'

'Do you think so?' she asked doubtfully.

Next morning there was a letter from Aunt Mabel. It read:

Dear Ellie and Alice,

I'm writing to you to let you know that your mam gave birth to an eight-pound baby boy last week. We were all in tears at the sight of him because he is the image of your dad, and he is to be christened Matthew. Your mam is doing well. Peggy and I are taking good care of her. She will be going back to the cottage as soon as she is up and about because Ed is home, thankfully. He is taking good care of the farm, and keeping company with a nice girl from the far side of Lisheen.

We miss you both, but knowing that you are in a better place is a comfort to all of us. Write and let us know all of your news.

Love

Mabel

'Just think, we have a baby brother, and he's growing bigger every day, and we're not there to see him,' Alice said. 'He'll be practically grown up when we do see him.'

That night, when I thought of his tiny hands curled into fists, his gummy smile as he lay in Mam's arms, I turned my face to the wall so that Alice wouldn't hear me cry.

I was wondering how I could afford the material for the dresses on the meagre two dollars a week pocket money I got from Aunt Sally when I dropped a plate, one of the good Crown Derby ones, a wedding present from Aunt

Sally's family. It smashed into smithereens. Eamon came quickly to see what had happened. 'What have you done?' he said, when he saw me picking up the pieces, adding nastily, 'You'll have to pay for it out of your wages, you know.'

Something in me snapped and I threw a piece of broken crockery at him. It hit the side of his head, cutting him. He went for me, twisting my arms. 'You've gone too far this time.' He stormed off, blood seeping from the cut. I swept up the china, my knees quaking, wrapped it in newspaper and put it in the bin.

That night I lay thinking of all the people sleeping in the house, and how most of us, particularly the lodgers, were just strangers, passing daily on the stairs; we meant nothing to each other. Except for Eamon, who was making it his business to get in my way. He would creep around the house as though he was spying on me. Walking the corridors, pushing open a door, I would listen for his step, feel my heart lurch with panic at any odd, disconnected sound. Whichever room I entered, he always seemed to be nearby, sometimes appearing from nowhere and staring at me, transfixed. I never knew what time he came into the house, or what time he left – but even when he was out, the house seemed to be full of him.

Bridget was wrong not to place any importance on Eamon's behaviour. I knew that if I stayed long enough he would make life intolerable for me.

Often, after I'd finished housework for the day a new, strange aloneness took me roaming the streets, to find my bearings. I went to the quiet, tree-lined square nearby. Another time I took myself off to the small brightly painted shops in Little Italy where every kind of Italian food was on sale. Swarms of people were hurrying by, all wrapped up against the cold. There were people in doorways, in rattling buses, in taxis and cars, on bicycles. I was enthralled by so many streets, clumped in what were called 'blocks', all tight together, and crammed with shops, and bars.

One day Bridget told me to run some errands. 'Don't rush back,' she said, with a smile. So when I'd finished shopping for her I took the subway to Central Park. I walked with the crowds up Broadway to Times Square, marvelling at the electric signs, the movie houses, the hawkers on the sidewalks, the orange-juice vendor. I bought a street map and a hot dog and walked to Fifty-Ninth Street. I stood at the intersection, astonished at the network of streets and the crowds of people. This was the exciting life that I'd craved while listening to Aunt Mabel's stories. This was the New York of my dreams.

Outside the Plaza hotel rows of cars were parked: Dodge, Buick, Packard written on their gleaming bonnets. Horse-drawn carriages driven by top-hatted coachmen with Irish accents were lined up outside the gates of Central Park.

Inside the park, people were strolling along in the afternoon sunshine. I sat on a bench by the boating pool and watched children rowing around the little lake in tiny boats. Slipping off my shoes and socks I bathed my aching feet in the water, as cool and silky as our river back home. In Ireland the creamy primroses would be scattered among the hedgerows, choking by now with hawthorn. The purple heather would be blooming on the hills. I closed my eyes and imagined our cottage drab and deserted-looking, the grass around it high, the red honeysuckle growing wild on the hedgerows surrounding it. I thought of Ed and wondered if the civil war was over yet.

I was mentally composing a letter to Mam, telling her all about this magical city and my adventures, when the snap of fallen twigs caused me to look round and catch a shape in the nearby trees. I was sure it was Eamon and I looked away, fearful. When I turned back he had gone. Perhaps it had been a trick of the light, or my over-active imagination, but whatever it was I decided not to tempt fate by hanging around, so I made my way back to the subway station.

With a heavy heart I returned to the underground, not wanting to leave Manhattan. In the dusk the stores were all lit up. Rows of lights shone from the skyscrapers; there were blue flashes from the elevated trains and the lights of cars stretched as far as the eye could see.

As soon as I walked through the door, Aunt Sally pounced on me.

'Where have you been?' Her eyes scorched me.

'Central Park,' Eamon said, coming into the hall.

'Central Park!' she screamed at me. 'Do you realise how dangerous it is to walk there alone, never mind loiter?'

'It seemed quite safe to me.'

'Anything could have happened to you. You cannot be trusted. You're barred from going to the shops again,' she ranted.

Alice and Mary-Pat were doing their homework, Mary-Pat called to me. 'We'd like some sandwiches for our supper,' she said. 'Bridget's gone to bed with a headache and there's no one to make them for us.'

Wearily, I made them their sandwiches and said, 'I think you should go to bed now, it's late.'

'Bossy boots,' Mary-Pat said cheekily. 'You're only the maid.'

I was cleaning in one of the bedrooms when Eamon appeared out of nowhere. He came towards me, put his hand on my neck, and pushed me against the wall. I ducked away from him. He grabbed me and pulled me towards him.

'Let go,' I hissed.

'Or you'll do what?' he smirked, tightening his grip on me.

He pulled me into his room, where he jerked my

head back, forcing me to look at him. 'Let yourself go,' he said, swinging me round, pushing me up against the wall. I opened my mouth to scream. He covered it with his hand, and tightened his grip on me. I struggled, but my strength was no match for his. I glanced around to see if there was anything I could grab to hit him with. He was tugging at my clothes in a frenzied way, breathing heavily. If he'd only let go of me just for a second I might have a chance to spring up. I looked towards the door, hoping desperately that someone would come to my rescue. All this time his eyes were on me. I lifted my elbows up and pushed into his chest with all my strength. He coughed, grabbed my shoulders, and slammed me back against the wall. Suddenly, the door opened and Aunt Sally strode in. Eamon let me go so quickly that I stumbled backwards, breathless. Relief flooded through me as I saw Aunt Sally's white, stricken face. For the first time since I'd met her I was glad to see her. Now she would see what her precious son was really like.

'What were you doing?' she said, outraged, glaring from Eamon to me.

Eamon, eyes never wavering, said innocently, 'I was trying to get Ellie out of here. She's been stealing my books.'

Aunt Sally drew herself up and walked directly over to me. 'In my bedroom now, this minute,' she shouted.

Without a backward glance at Eamon I followed her.

'I will not tolerate this behaviour,' she huffed as soon as her bedroom door was closed. I've noticed you following Eamon around. From now on the loft is out of bounds to you.' As my mouth opened in astonishment she began a lecture on morals, ending it threatening to write a letter of complaint to Mam.

'I'll give you one more chance, that's all,' she said. 'Any more of your carry-on and you'll be punished severely. Now go wash up and get ready to serve the dinner.'

Later, as Bridget handed me a plate of lamb stew and new potatoes she looked at me knowingly, but said nothing.

I was miserable. I hated Aunt Sally and I hated Eamon even more. There was no let up in their unfair treatment of me. I knew I had only to write a letter to Aunt Mabel, tell her of my predicament, and she would call Uncle Jack. Mam had her hands full with her new baby and a letter like that would only cause upset and concern. But truly, pride prevented me writing to her. Despite my loneliness, I didn't want to be told to go back home. I still wanted to go my own way, to discover life for myself, though I realised that I couldn't stay here with Aunt Sally and Eamon looming over me.

I'd have to think of a way to escape. If running away were the price for my freedom, I would pay it. And I knew that Bridget was on my side. She had suffered much the same hardship in the past.

One morning she said cheerfully, 'I have another letter for you.' Taking it out of her overall pocket, she smiled as she held it out to me. My eyes scanned the unfamiliar handwriting.

Dear Ellie

I hope this letter finds you and Alice as well as it leaves us all here. I promised your mam that I would keep you informed on things here. The sheep are doing well and the sale of the lambs was better than expected, I am glad to say. The fishing is good too, and this year's crop is promising, as there has been no rain for a couple of weeks.

Write and let me know how you are getting on. I wish you were here for the dancing at the crossroads. I miss you.

I remain,

Your faithful friend,

Johnny

I was thrilled to hear from him, and wrote back to him telling him everything – about Aunt Sally and Uncle Jack, Alice and Bridget. I didn't talk of Eamon – I knew it would make Johnny angry – but I did tell him how I longed to leave and find a real future for myself. It was such a relief to tell all my thoughts to someone I trusted. But as I finished the letter, I begged him not to mention a word of it to Mam or Aunt Mabel.

A plan was starting to form in my head, and the last thing I needed was a summons back home.

Ten

Now that the idea of leaving had hatched itself, I wondered if I could stand another minute in Aunt Sally's household. My feelings were mostly to do with my Aunt's and Eamon's strange behaviour towards me, but also with the strained relationship that existed between Uncle Jack and Aunt Sally.

In Eamon's presence Uncle Jack was cold and stern, and Eamon seemed to have little affection for him in return. Thankfully Eamon had taken to staying in his bedroom much of the day – or he would go out for hours on end. When he was there he would strut about, cocksure of himself. He continued his habit of casually bumping into me and giving me one of his malevolent glances, as if he were plotting some fiendish mischief. He scared me, but the thought of leaving and never seeing him again kept me going. I was determined to put on a show, be as civil as I could stand to my cousin while I was here.

One evening, Eamon returned late and cornered me in the passage, all smiles. 'You should come out with me one time, Eleanor,' he said, silkily. 'You could steal out when they are all in bed. They would never know. Once Mom is in her room with her bottle of gin, the house could fall down around her and she wouldn't know or care. And Dad sleeps like a log.'

'Thank you, but I don't think that's a good idea,' I said calmly.

'Oh really,' he sneered. 'You may seem innocent but I know different.'

'What do you mean?'

'You have a boyfriend back home.'

'I do not.'

'Mom showed me the letter he wrote you.'

So he and Aunt Sally had been reading my letters. I went to my room and re-read the letter that had given Eamon and Aunt Sally such bad-minded ideas. Johnny had written: 'I wish you were here for the dancing at the crossroads. I miss you.' Into that sentence they'd drawn their own conclusions.

I pushed past Eamon and ran up to my room, where I sat on my bed and wept. I felt that I was at the bottom of a great hole, unable to climb out of it. In the bathroom I splashed water on my face, and leaned over the sink, exhausted. I wondered if Johnny had received my letter to him yet, and if he would get back in touch.

A couple of weeks later there was a letter waiting there for me.

Dear Ellie

I was sorry to hear you are faring so badly. You are right to get away. I can't understand why you are being treated in this way, and why you haven't made your escape already. What's stopping you? You are young and strong, you can go anywhere in the world you feel like, and you have the guts to strike out on your own. Go ahead and do it.

I enclose five pounds: money left over from the sale of the last of your Mam's lambs. Should you find yourself in difficulties write to me at once and I will wire you some more money. Alice will be grand and fine without you. She seems to have fallen on her feet with the relatives.

Good luck, and write back and let me know where you are.

I remain,

Your faithful friend,

Johnny

Johnny was right. There was nothing to stop me going, especially now that I had the extra cash. That would get me by. I would have to go out and earn some money after that. I warned Bridget of my plans, filling her in on Eamon's latest behaviour.

'That boy!' she fumed. 'What's it all about?

I shook my head. 'I don't know, Bridget. I can't possibly stay here. Life is impossible for me.'

Bridget put her arm around me. 'I know, Eleanor, I know,' she said sadly. 'I'll do whatever I can to help you.'

Bridget had said that there were plenty of jobs to be

had – where all that was needed was physical strength. But where would I go? I knew nothing at all about any of the states in America – they were just names in coloured squares on Uncle Jack's globe. Then I remembered Violet and her invitation to visit her in Boston. I had her address still hidden in one of my stockings in the drawer. It was the lifeline that I needed. I thought of Zak who, by now, was becoming a more shadowy figure and less easy to remember. I closed my eyes the better to think about him. He would certainly not be thinking about me, and probably would be taken up with his job at the bank.

But despite my uncertainty I began to give Boston some serious thought. Knowing that Johnny was fully supportive of my decision to go made me feel stronger. I wrote to him, telling him that I'd decided to leave New York, and asking him not to tell Mam or Aunt Mabel. I promised to write to him again as soon as I had a new address.

Eleven

Some of the lodgers went home for Christmas; others went to stay with relatives. So the house was quiet and there were fewer chores to do. Aunt Mabel sent Alice and I some lovely clothes that she'd made for us, and Mam sent us two pound notes each with which to buy ourselves presents. Johnny sent me a frilly Christmas card with a pound note tucked inside it.

On Christmas Day, Aunt Sally stayed in bed with a bad cold. Alice and I helped Bridget with the cooking, while Uncle Jack and Eamon went for a walk. We decorated the dining-room table with sweets and crackers and we all ate together, including Bridget.

At the end of February I wrote Violet a letter, telling her that I was planning a visit to her. I didn't mention Aunt Sally and Uncle Jack or the awful situation, but asked her to write back to me at the post office address. My heart hurt at the thought of leaving Alice, though I knew she was secure and happy.

I got a letter back within a week. Violet was delighted to hear from me. She wrote that I should come and stay with her and her family as soon as I liked, and for as long as I liked.

Next day I went to the train station, where I discovered that the passenger train from New York to Boston departed each afternoon at three o'clock, taking the shoreline route through Brooklyn and Long Island, stopping at New Haven and Willimantic and some smaller stations along the way. What could be easier than taking a train from Brooklyn?

When I got back I replied to Violet's letter, thanking her for her kind invitation and giving her the date and time of my arrival. As there had been no mention of Zak in her letter, I decided not to mention him either.

From then on I worked like a demon in an effort to win Aunt Sally's approval and put her off the scent. Even she couldn't fail to admire my diligence. One Thursday I said to her, 'Bridget has some extra errands for me to do tomorrow, I may be back late.' There was silence, but no objection from Aunt Sally.

My plans were made. For the rest of the day I began to feel a sense of restriction and restlessness as the time went slowly by.

That night in bed, I was scared and excited all at once. With so many hurdles ahead of me I hardly slept. I'd never been on a train before, but as I finally drifted off to sleep I made up my mind that no matter how scared I was I was going to take that journey.

★ ★ ★

As soon as the alarm clock went off next morning I was up out of bed. After I'd served breakfast I waved Alice and Mary-Pat off to school with a cheery goodbye, my heart breaking as I watched them bounce happily down the road. When my chores were done I sadly said goodbye to Bridget, took my tiny cloth bag containing all I was taking with me, and left the house while Aunt Sally was having her nap. I walked quickly along the pavement, and out of sight.

It was a chill day. There were lots of people out shopping in the local small stores. I bumped into Mrs Dean, one of Aunt Sally's friends, who had come to the house once or twice. My heart pounded as she stopped me.

'Where are you off to?' she asked pleasantly, but with genuine curiosity.

'I have to run a few errands for Bridget,' I said, with as much composure as I could manage. She nodded and I darted past her to the end of the block, dreading every step I heard behind me. I knew Mrs Dean would tell Aunt Sally she'd seen me, but my story was straight. I just had to get as far away as possible before it dawned on Aunt Sally that I'd run away. I felt a tightening fear in my chest, but I had to go through with it.

I walked quickly on through the streets that bordered the railway line, crossed the footbridge, thudded down the steps, and ran along the path on the side of the railway, past bushes, and discarded rubbish. By the time I reached the station, I was in a state of near terror and had a stitch in my side from walking so fast. I found the ticket hall, bought a one-way ticket to Boston, and waited for the train, not daring to wonder what would happen if Violet didn't show up to meet me.

When I saw the long, black locomotive snaking into the station, its horn shrieking like a stuck-pig, smoke billowing from its sides, I walked to the far end of the station before I summoned up the courage to board it. The harsh rattle of the doors shutting sent shudders through the carriages as the train set off slowly with another shrill blast. Everything seemed to go quiet except for the slow grinding of the wheels on the track.

I breathed out at last, grateful to be on my way, and settled down into my seat. The train slowed a little as it pulled further away from the station and passed the footbridge I had come across minutes before. My heart lurched as I spotted a familiar figure on the bridge. Eamon! He seemed to be staring directly down at me; his hands clenched into fists, his shoulders lifting like a threat. On legs like jelly, I jumped up and ran practically the length of the train, my cheeks burning, thinking he would suddenly leap on me with cries of 'Gottcha'.

I took a seat in an end carriage, filled with people, and watched with a pounding heart the sunlight falling through the black miles of track as we gathered speed.

The city drifted past as the train chugged through tunnels and around bends. When it pulled into the next station my pulse had finally slowed, and the fear that Eamon might suddenly appear beside me subsided. Even so, when a bag thumped down next to me at one stop, for a few seconds I waited, tense with expectation that he would appear and grab me. But it was a stranger who sat down on the seat by my side, of course.

It was only when we were finally out in the countryside that I properly relaxed. Wide sloping fields appeared, horses grazing here and there in the slanting sunshine. Occasionally, a solitary farmhouse would fly by and I would wonder who lived in it. Here and there workers toiled, their shadows bent to the golden fields. Looking at them I had a sense of home. I closed my eyes to the rumbling of the train and slept. I dreamed of our cottage; its image rose up before me so real that as I reached out to touch the whitewashed wall I woke with a start, my eyes damp with tears.

As we raced past the little towns nestled in rough pastures, the train grew so cold that I had to squeeze down into my coat to keep warm. Soon, instead of endless fields, cable wires and telegraph poles appeared. The tracks increased, and clumps of houses came into view, then streets, and traffic. We were in Boston.

I clambered out and, with a surge of energy, ran up the steps, hoping that Violet would be waiting for me. As I emerged into the ice-cold station a fur-clad figure came striding towards me through a cloud of smoke that belched from the train, her shiny hair swinging in a new French bob. There was delight in her face at seeing me again.

'Ellie! There you are!' She held out her arms.

'Violet!' I rushed into them.

Violet swept me out of the station, and soon we were in a cab driving through a succession of streets and she began flinging questions at me. 'Are you OK? Did you find the journey long?'

'I think you're going to like it here,' she said. 'It's not quite as busy as New York but it's fun. I'm going to help you settle in, and there's a dinner-dance tomorrow night. I've put you in the room next door to mine!' she said excitedly.

For the first time in weeks my loneliness ebbed away. 'I'm glad to be here Violet, and very grateful,' I said, meaning every word.

Each turn the cab took had fewer streetlights. Then Violet said, 'This is our street,' as we turned up a curvy, tree-lined road and pulled into a driveway.

'Violet! It's lovely!' I exclaimed, opening the car door.

'Come on, let's go inside,' she smiled.

Violet's family lived in a large apartment on two storeys. It was as big as a house, and warm and welcoming. As we walked through the front door a tall man in a dark suit came to greet me. 'You must be Eleanor,' he said, his eyes crinkling as he took my hand in his. 'I'm Violet's father, and I'm very pleased to meet you. Come on in and make yourself at home.'

Violet's mother was a sweet woman with big round eyes like Violet's. She took my hand. 'I'm so glad you are here, dear. Violet has told me all about you.'

'Thank you, Mrs Kelleher,' I said.

'Let me show you to your room, Ellie,' Violet said, leading me up a flight of stairs, along a corridor to a small room with blue-and-white flowered wallpaper, a blue carpet to match. There was a single bed with a patchwork quilt on it, a small table and chair, and a dressing table.

'It's grand,' I said.

Violet beamed. 'Good,' she said proudly. 'And here is your bathroom.' She opened the door to a small bathroom with cool blue walls.

'Oh, Violet, this is perfect, thank you!' I exclaimed, trying to take it all in.

'You're welcome, I'll leave you to put your things away . . .' Her eyes fell on my forlorn cloth bag. 'When you've washed up come downstairs. You must be hungry,' she said.

As soon as she'd gone I sat on the bed and removed my boots, resting my aching feet on the deep carpeting. I hung my coat in the closet, then took out of my bag my few clothes and hung them up. I put my wash bag and hairbrush in the bathroom.

That night, the apartment was quiet. It was pitch-dark

outside my bedroom window except for a blade of light that shone through the curtains in the house opposite, casting a ghostly glow on the lawn. Beyond that there was just an almost black sky dotted with a few stars. I knelt down at the side of my bed to say a prayer for Alice, then slid under the covers.

As soon as I closed my eyes Eamon's angry image came into my head, his threatening figure looming over me. I sat bolt upright in bed, opening my eyes to find nothing but the still darkness of my room. Reassured, I lay back down and snuggled into my pillows, knowing that I was out of Eamon's reach.

Someone was knocking at my door, calling my name.

'Ellie!'

I rubbed my eyes, pushed back the covers and jumped out of bed. 'Come in! I'm awake!' I called.

Violet opened the door, a mug of coffee in her hand. She passed it to me. 'Come on downstairs when you're ready,' she said, with a reassuring smile.

When I found the kitchen – a large room with white walls and pots of cactuses, along with other strange-looking plants – Violet was sitting at the long table toasting bread for breakfast. A pot of coffee steamed on the table, and a basket of hardboiled eggs sat beside various jams and marmalades. I helped myself, and ate ravenously.

As we breakfasted, Violet's eyes were full of concern.

'Look at your hands,' she said, clasping one. 'All rough from work.' She squeezed it tighter. 'Tell me all about it, Ellie.'

When I'd finished recounting my time in the boarding house, Violet shook her head in disbelief. She squeezed my hand again. 'You've had an awful time. But you're safe now, and that's all that matters.'

'It's very kind of you to have me here, but I can't stay here for ever,' I said, gratefully. 'I must find a place . . . get a job . . .'

'I'll help you,' Violet promised. Her compassion was so different from the angry-faced dismissive Aunt Sally, who obviously believed that a deprived life was character building. It was as though I had stepped from a nightmare into a dream.

After breakfast we walked for miles around Boston, as Violet showed me the sights. We walked along Hanover Street, where there were grocery stores, bakeries and restaurants and, further along, beautiful residential houses.

'Boston is the best city in the world. You're going to love it here Ellie,' Violet said with conviction.

She was right. Already I was falling in love with it.

Twelve

That evening, I was sitting on Violet's balcony, thinking of Alice, wondering how she was getting along without me, when a shadow fell across my chair. I looked up to find Zak standing in front of me, his eyes wide and friendly.

'Eleanor!' He held out his hand for mine and clasped it warmly. I felt myself flushing with pleasure and surprise. I'd dreamed of this meeting, of hearing him speak my name again, and here he was with the same smouldering eyes and quirky smile. And he looked wonderful, even more handsome than I'd remembered. The sunlight made his amber eyes startlingly clear.

'Hello Zak.' I made a deliberate effort to sound casual.

He pulled a chair out next to me and sat down. 'I couldn't wait to get here – ever since Violet said that you were coming. I hope you're staying for a while.'

'Yes, I hope so too,' I said, and I meant it, more than ever now.

Zak looked thoughtful. 'I hope you don't mind, but Violet told me a little of what happened . . . at your uncle's place.' He paused. 'They had no intention of sending you to college, had they?'

I shook my head. 'I made a terrible mistake in thinking that they would,' I admitted, feeling a little ashamed for some reason.

Zak reached out for my hand again. 'It wasn't your fault, Ellie, you mustn't brood on it.' He smiled. 'The question is, do you regret coming to America after the bad start you've had here?'

'No, I don't think so.' I cleared my throat. 'I wanted to get away . . .' I hesitated. 'After my father drowned.'

'Your father drowned?' Zak looked shaken.

I nodded, trying not to cry again.

'I'm so sorry. Why did you never mention it before?' he asked, leaning towards me, taking my hand.

'It was hard to talk about it.' My voice cracked. I hung my head as I remembered watching Dad's limp body being lifted off Sheerin's boat.

'Oh Eleanor!' said Zak.

I looked up into his face and saw the concern in his eyes. 'We'll help you in any way we can. What about your sister?'

At the mention of her name I felt such sorrow that I couldn't hide it. 'I hated leaving her behind, but Aunt Sally and Uncle Jack love her,' I told him. 'She's company for their only daughter, Mary-Pat.' I stared at my hands, wondering if she was sitting and waiting for me to come home, trying to figure out where I'd gone.

As if reading my thoughts, Zak said, 'She'll be fine. From what you say she seems happy, and she's getting plenty of attention. At her age all you care about is what you want.'

That evening, after dinner, Zak said, 'Would you like to go for a stroll, find your bearings?'

'I'd love to,' I said, getting to my feet.

We walked to the Charles River and crossed over the bridge. People were milling around, out for enjoyment, but it felt as if it were just the two of us. We wandered on down to the waterfront, drifting along with the crowd. Sailors with tattoos on their arms sat on a wall, talking and laughing. A feeling of contentment finally flooded through me as we stood gazing down into the inky water. Shimmering pools of light reflected on its surface. Boats rocked gently in their moorings. The air was cold. Zak touched my arm and said, 'I'm glad you're here, Ellie.' The huskiness in his voice made me go weak at the knees. 'What about a nightcap?' he said, taking my arm.

The coffee shop was almost empty. Zak led me to a vacant table at the dark end. A waiter appeared, and Zak ordered a soda for me and a small whiskey for himself. We chatted on, as we watched boats sailing on the shimmering water outside.

A fine drizzle was falling as we left the café, and we hurried back, laughing. As we ran past a bar, music flowed out, making us link arms and slow down a little.

Stars appeared in the sky, the moonlight bathed Zak's face. 'Ellie, I hate to think of all those bad things happening to you. We must make you happy again.'

'I'm happy now. Tell me about all the wonderful things that are going on in your life,' I said, smiling.

Zak glanced towards the blurred glow of the city lights. 'Every one of my friends is falling in love. It's becoming a kind of epidemic.'

I laughed. 'Are you afraid of falling in love?'

'Me! Oh no, no.' He leaned towards me flirtatiously. 'What about you, have you met any nice boys in New York?'

I thought of Eamon and shivered. I had no intention of telling Zak about him. 'Lord no! You are the only boy I've met since I left Ireland.'

Zak looked at me with a strange expression in his eyes and I knew he was going to kiss me. His eager lips were soft and inviting. I pressed my mouth to his. Suddenly the world stood still. Pulling me close, he kissed me again, harder, until we were both breathless and dizzy.

On the way back to Violet's he held my hand possessively, and I couldn't believe I was here with him. Even Aunt Sally and Eamon became shadowy, unimportant figures.

Zak didn't come in, but promised to see me soon again.

'Where do you live?' I asked him.

'I have an apartment nearby.' He looked at me with a

strange expression in his eyes as he said, 'I'm glad you're staying on. I never want you to go far away again. Promise me you never will.'

'I promise.'

'Good.' He kissed me softly. 'I'll see you Friday evening.'

As we parted. I felt as if I was floating on air.

Violet was still up when I went in. 'You're looking lovely tonight, Ellie. How did you get on with Zak?'

I blushed.

'You're falling for him. I can see it in your eyes,' she said gleefully.

I went to bed. Closing the door softly behind me I looked into the mirror. My eyes were shining, my skin glowing, and my lips were bruised from Zak's kiss. I thought of Alice alone in her bedroom and wished I could tell her about all the wonderful things that were happening to me.

The following afternoon, Zak took me to the common and the park. The sun was shining; people were out enjoying the good weather. Hand in hand we strolled in the shade of willow trees. The sheer joy of walking beside him made every nerve in my body tingle. Everywhere was coloured with a dream-like glow. I was filled with intense energy and a happiness that invaded every space of my being.

Zak said, 'Boston is beautiful, don't you agree?'

It was enchanting, and it was ours. It belonged to us. We walked along, exploring without a care. Zak enjoyed sharing his old haunts with me.

'When we were kids we spent every minute in these parks. We used to pretend that this was the jungle, and that we were chasing wild animals,' he laughed, pointing to a group of trees and bushes. 'Hard to believe that wild horses roamed here once,' he said, an excited expression in his eyes.

We sat on a bench and watched baby mallards following in their mother's wake, quacking and splashing on the glassy water. At the corner we listened to the passionate preaching of an evangelist. 'Just imagine, George Washington and Benjamin Franklin walked right here,' Zak said. He talked about the famous Boston Tea Party and about the slavery on the Underground Railroad, the oldest subway system in the world. As he spoke, I took in the intricate architecture of the Beacon Hill brownstones and the gold-domed Massachusetts State House, glittering in the sunshine, while soaking up his tales.

I envied him his childhood, glimpsing a much more interesting and exotic one than my own had been so far. Zak's self-confidence and graciousness made me feel my lack of education keenly. I remarked on this to him, but he only smiled and told me not to be silly.

The next day we went to the Public Garden and strolled along its meandering paths and manicured beds exploding with fragrant roses. We walked on over the tiny footbridge that replicated Brooklyn Bridge. I was so glad I wasn't in New York any more. The earthy, damp smell under the weeping willow trees reminded me of summer evenings at home. I said, 'It's like Ireland here — without the cattle, of course. I never thought that I could like a place so much.'

Zak reached for my hand. 'And I never thought I could like a girl so much.' He leaned across and kissed me. It was a respectful kiss. We smiled at each other, locked into the moment. Then we pulled back, suddenly remembering that we were in a public place. I watched the shake of Zak's shoulders as he laughed.

'By the way, I won't be able to see you until next weekend,' he said as we strolled back to Violet's.

'Are you going away?'

'I'll be spending a few weeks in an investment bank in Washington as part of my training course. Didn't Violet say?'

'No . . .' I could feel my heart drop like a stone.

'Don't worry. I'll be back weekends, you'll see plenty of me then.' In the lamplight his eyes were bright and sincere. 'Meanwhile, Violet will take good care of you.'

Feeling foolish, I assured him that I'd be busy job-hunting, but the thought of us having to part for another week made me feel sad.

★ ★ ★

I scanned the advertising columns in the Boston Globe for a week without results. There were plenty of jobs for ladies' maids and sales clerks, but nothing that suited me.

Then one morning I spotted an advertisement that read: *Wanted: Seamstress for Shirt Factory*.

I held the page out excitedly to Violet. 'This job sounds perfect. I could improve my sewing skills.'

'It would do for a start,' she agreed.

I applied, and received a letter by return of post requesting me to attend an interview on the following Monday morning. Violet was delighted when I told her.

Early on the Monday, I took the trolley car to Downtown North End and walked to the factory, a huge hangar hidden behind a dilapidated warehouse, with four narrow windows facing an alleyway. It was all comings and goings. Vans arrived and left.

Inside, telephones rang ceaselessly as I stood nervously outside a door marked 'Office' before I plucked up the courage to knock on it.

A tall, strict-looking woman came out of it.

'Hello, my name is Eleanor O'Rourke. I'm here for a job interview,' I said.

She smiled tightly. 'I'm Miss Flint, the Floor Lady, come in. Have you worked in a factory before?'

'No, I haven't, but I know how to use a sewing machine.'

She looked at me doubtfully. 'The work we produce

here is top quality'. She opened the door of a large cabinet behind her desk and took out a pile of shirts. 'These are the kind of shirts we make,' she said proudly.

There were shirts made of sheer linen and the finest flannel. She brought out more shirts: silk ones this time, in blue, apple-green, lavender and pale pink, some monogrammed in dark blue thread on the pockets.

'I've never seen such beautiful shirts,' I exclaimed.

'And you won't see them anywhere else. We pride ourselves on our designs and fine stitching,' she said imperiously. 'Now I'll show you around.'

She led me to a corner of the factory, where silent girls in white overalls were standing at long tables, unrolling lengths of the fabrics and slitting them expertly across the cutting table with the points of their shears. The air around them was thick with snowy fibres that danced in the light.

'These girls have a knack of judging exactly how many garments each length of material will make, so that there's no waste,' Miss Flint said.

'We have to make sure we're getting the most out of each bale,' a tall girl said, heaving a length on to the cutting table.

Turning away, Miss Flint said, 'Now, let's see how you handle a sewing machine.' She led me to a long table where six girls worked at bench in their coats, all sewing lengths of linen on big, black industrial machines, and sat me down in front of one. Handing me a length of linen, she said, 'We'll start you off on the side seams. See how you handle this monster.'

I spun the handle. It squeaked. 'Needs a little oil,' she said, dabbing some here and there. It smelled of axle grease as it ran along a length of linen in a perfect straight line. Miss Flint looked approvingly at my work.

'Good. When can you start?' she asked, a pleased expression on her face.

'Now, if you like.'

Miss Flint smiled. 'Great! Shirlee'll show you what to do.' The pretty girl next to me with flaxen hair tied up in a scarf and a couldn't-care-less look in her big blue eyes, stood up from her machine. 'Shirlee, this is Eleanor. I want you to take charge of her.'

'Yes, ma'am.' Turning to me, she said, 'Howdy! Nice to meet ya, Eleanor,' shaking my hand, her smile lighting up her face.

'Call me Ellie,' I said to her as soon as Miss Flint left, and I went to take my coat off.

Shirlee said, 'Keep it on, y'all freeze otherwise. That wall behind you is ice-cold. Now, Mr Samuel is always complaining that wearing our coats hinders our work.'

'He's always sayin' that the work's not going out fast enough,' a gum-chewing girl next to her said. 'We've told him to give us more heat, or we'll walk out on him.'

'This is Dora,' Shirlee said. 'She's a fighter.'

'Don't have no choice,' Dora said with a wicked grin.

I sewed the lengths of linen Shirlee gave me quickly,

and waited for the next lot. When I started on the silk material, the machine raced ahead and got stuck. I tried to push the silk through the jabbering machine but it wouldn't budge. 'Damn,' I swore under my breath.

'Don't fret yourself,' Shirlee said, and tried to unravel it, without success. 'It's the damn machine. It's ancient.' She called out, 'Miss Flint!'

Miss Flint came over. 'What is it?' she asked.

'There's something wrong with Ellie's machine,' Shirlee told her.

'What have you done to it?' asked Miss Flint in a condescending tone, as if she were talking to a very small child.

'I don't know, Ma'am,' I said defensively.

'It's the machine, it's useless,' Shirlee said pointedly.

'Let me see,' Miss Flint said crossly.

I stood up and let her sit down. She tried to turn the wheel but couldn't. She unravelled the bobbin. 'Look, see that pin, it's stuck in there. You should have taken it out of the material,' she explained, releasing it; and bundling it up and getting to her feet, she stuffed it in the waste bin. 'Don't let it happen again,' she said as she walked off.

'Take no notice of her, she's harmless,' Shirlee said, pulling a face that made me laugh.

It was boring work sewing straight seams all day long, but we were allowed a break for ten minutes during which I sat with the other girls and drank coffee. When

I told them that I'd just arrived from Ireland they were much more welcoming, asking me all about the 'oul sod'.

The depot drivers passed in and out, picking up consignments. The girls called them in and joked with them. I felt shy in their presence and kept my eyes down.

When the lunch bell rang, Shirlee got to her feet. 'Come on, let's go get somethin' to eat. Ma belly's stuck to ma backbone.' She got me coffee from a machine in the canteen, then took me out to the yard where she shared her sandwiches with me, sitting on a wall. A couple of the other machinists joined us and plied me with questions.

'Where did you learn to sew so good?'

'My Aunt Mabel taught me. She's a milliner. She trained with Jeffrey Rowe in New York,' I told them.

'Did she teach y'all how to make hats?' Shirlee asked.

'Yes, she did,' I said proudly.

'Really!' Dora asked, wide-eyed. 'So, what're you doin' here sewin' straight seams?'

'It's just until I get myself an apprenticeship,' I said.

'I'm only here for a while,' Shirlee said. '. . . I can quit this god-awful job any time I want to.'

The other girls tittered.

'You wouldn't quit. You're just sayin' that,' Dora said.

On the way back, Miss Flint called out to us to hold our backs straight. 'You're all walkin' like sacks of potatoes,' she yelled.

'She's a dope, that Miss Flint,' Shirlee said, and laughed a big, throaty laugh.

That evening, as soon as we'd all clocked off, I dashed back to Violet's, impatient to tell her all about my first day's work.

Thirteen

Each morning I walked down the empty streets with my packed lunch to face the long day ahead. At work, as the weather warmed up, I pushed the heavy wheel of my machine grateful for the cold wall at my back to cool me down. The constant whirring noise around me set my ears buzzing but I did my job to the best of my ability. My energy increased with the workload, and I impressed Miss Flint with my diligence.

While I worked, I thought of Alice and wondered how she was coping without me there to protect her. I wondered about Mam, Lucy and what Matthew, our new baby brother looked like. I considered writing to Johnny Sheerin to ask him for all the news of home, but decided against it for fear he'd let slip my whereabouts to anybody. By the time I left the factory each evening, my head was spinning with fatigue and my arms and back ached.

One morning, a young gentleman in a dark suit, over-starched shirt and patent leather shoes came into the factory. He was handsome in a serious sort of way, with a jutting jaw and sharp eyes. 'Good mornin' ladies,' he greeted us, swaying slightly.

Shirlee jumped up and almost ran to him. 'What can I do for you, Mr Samuel?' she asked.

'I hear complaints about that last batch of shirts,' he said, his eyes flickering appreciatively over Shirlee.

'Well,' said Miss Flint, crossing the room. 'That won't happen again. I've checked all of these and they're perfect.' She cast a disapproving look at Shirlee, who went back to her machine, earning a last admiring glance from Mr Samuel.

'That's Mr Samuel,' whispered Shirlee. 'He's the boss's son. Honest,' she said. 'He's a swell-looking fella, don't ya think? Every time I see him walk in here my heart flips over.' She leaned towards me. 'Can you imagine being married to a man who owns a factory?'

'He doesn't own it yet,' one of the other girls corrected her.

'But he will one day . . . so what's the difference,' Shirlee said lightly.

'Girls, be quiet!' called Miss Flint. 'Mr Samuel has something to say to us all.' She stepped aside as Mr Samuel cleared his throat and announced that he was about to select the winner of the Seamstress of the Year Award. All the girls sat up straight. Shirlee gave him a particularly flirtatious look.

'I'll be coming to a decision very soon,' he said finally. 'For now, you all carry on as you are, producing the very 'best high-quality garments.' He nodded at the listening throng, turned and left the room, followed by Miss Flint.

'Well,' said Shirlee jovially, 'what'd ya think everyone's gonna say when I win it?'

'How do you know you're going to win?' said Wilma, a mousy girl who envied Shirlee.

'Because Mr Samuel has a soft spot for me,' Shirlee confided. 'Didn't ya notice how he gave me the eye?'

The girls rolled their eyes and turned back to their machines.

My days fell into a routine. Work was exhausting and dull. I sewed seams until my head was spinning. I was glad of Shirlee, the life and soul of the factory, laughing and winking at the delivery boys who came and went. She did go on sometimes, and the only thing that protected her from getting into more trouble with Miss Flint was the fact that the finished work she produced was always excellent. I envied her her high spirits and love of life. Shirlee lived for the present. All I seemed to do was think of my future.

When Zak returned the following Saturday, he took me to the cinema to see *Sherlock Jr.* with Buster Keaton and Katheryn McGuire. With his carved features and aura of excitement, Buster was Zak's hero. Afterwards, over coffee, he invited me to a jazz concert the following week.

Panic-stricken, I said, 'I'd love to go, but I don't have a suitable frock to wear.'

'Violet'll take you shopping,' he said with a smile.

Deciding that I had leaned too much on her family's kindness, I told Violet that I would be finding my own place now that I was earning money. She implored me to stay longer, telling me that I was no trouble at all.

'Violet, you've been so kind to me, but I feel I have to stand on my own two feet,' I explained, hugging her.

'Well, if you're sure . . .' she said, a little sadly. 'But promise me we'll stay in constant contact!'

'I promise.'

The room I rented with my first week's wages was a narrow, third-floor back room in a dingy house. A window overlooked the back yard, and it was furnished with an iron bedstead, a wardrobe, a table, a small chest of drawers and a chair. A gas ring sat between the table and the chair, and the shared bathroom was down the corridor. The large window was a godsend. I opened it to let out some of the stale air and noticed the faded wallpaper and the slight damp in the cornices. The door was sticking, too. It was far from luxurious, but it was clean. It would do.

'With a little imagination,' said Violet, who had accompanied me to pay my deposit, 'I'm sure we can make it cosy . . .' though she looked around doubtfully.

On my first night, the noisy plumbing kept me awake. The house shuddered and creaked, and the smell of someone else's late-night cooking filtered up through the floorboards. I gave up on sleep and got up to look out of the window. The yard was full of tufted dirt, litter and old tyres, and an ancient bicycle toppled against the wall. The humid night meant that the heat settled everywhere. For the first time in my life I felt that I was really alone. Was I going to be alone like this for ever? Worse than that was the thought of going to the factory the next day, and every day after for a long time to come. I couldn't leave it; I was penniless, without contacts, and home was thousands of miles away.

One evening after work, I brought Shirlee home for tea. She could barely hide her shock at the cramped room and the rickety back yard.

'Ellie, why don't ya go home . . . back to your folks?' she said kindly. 'What's keeping you in this hell-hole?'

'I can't,' I said stubbornly. 'There's nothing in Ireland for me. This is where my future is – and anyway I'm not giving up now.'

It was true. I couldn't face returning home with nothing to show for my time in America. 'I'll never go back, Shirlee,' I said defiantly.

Fourteen

America, to me, was not the wonderful world of streets paved with gold and fortunes to be made that had been presented to me by Aunt Mabel. It was the America of a sixteen-year-old immigrant; a brow-beaten factory worker on the lowest of wages.

By day, as the factory echoed with the constant whirr of the machines, my fantasy of becoming a milliner began to grow. At night, I would go and sit by the window with my sketchpad and design my hats in the light from the streetlamp. Gradually, with my new sketches I became more confident. I started saving a few dollars here and there for a second-hand sewing machine. As soon as I could afford one, I'd get going on my own designs and work on them at night.

Violet took me to a small shop in Newbury Street, where frocks more divine than anything I'd ever seen before were on display. 'They're very expensive,' I said, checking the price tickets.

Undeterred, Violet picked out a dark blue silk dress

with a heart-shaped neckline. 'Try this one on,' she said.

In the tiny fitting room, I instantly fell in love with it. My skin looked soft, my eyes even darker than usual. I pinched my cheeks to make them glow, hating the dimples that appeared in them when I smiled, then smoothed back the tendrils of hair that curled round my face.

'You look very pretty,' Violet assured me as I did a twirl.

'I can't possibly afford it,' I said.

Going to the counter, standing in front of the till she said, 'I insist on buying it for you.'

I looked at her. 'I can't take it, I owe you so much already.'

She smiled. 'I want to indulge you, so let me. Some day, when you're rich and famous, you can indulge me.'

'What if it never happens?'

'It will,' she said, with conviction.

That evening, at Violet's, we put our hair up in curlers and gave each other a manicure. I put on some of her panstick, shaded my eyes a delicate blue, my lips a deep red, and was dressed in my new frock just as Zak arrived, with his friend, Gino, to pick us up. Gino, an attractive young man, with dark expressive eyes, and hands that waved about as he talked, drove to Jeepers, the new jazz club in the city centre.

Outside, a large crowd had formed. Zak took my

hand and we pushed forward. Jazz blared out as we went inside. The ceiling was studded with tiny fake stars. The orchestra played 'I Wanna Be Loved By You'. Zak whispered, 'Do you hear what they're singing?' I nodded, and looked up at him. 'Let's dance,' he said, tapping his feet impatiently, eyeing the dancing couples on the floor.

We were dancing the Charleston, swinging our arms, crossing them over our knees, having the time of our lives, when suddenly a girl with dark, expressive eyes and perfect cheekbones thrust herself forward. 'Hello Zak,' she called out.

'Gloria!' He took a step in her direction.

'I haven't seen you for ages, Zak,' she said flirtatiously.

'I was out of town,' he said to her, politely.

With a gleam in her eye she said, 'Call me. We'll go to tea.' Then she turned and danced away.

'Who's she?' I asked him when the music stopped.

'Just a girl I know,' Zak said with a shrug. 'Let's get a drink.'

With a sigh of relief, I followed him to the soda fountain.

But as the night wore on, I couldn't stop thinking about the girl, Gloria. Doubts about her surfaced later as we said goodnight. 'There's nothing between you and that girl?' I asked him.

'Of course not.' Looking away Zak added, in a strained voice, 'We went out a couple of times that's all.'

He seemed impatient at having to make this point.

Leaning towards him I said, 'I'm sorry, I don't know why I mentioned her. I shouldn't have.'

'Let's forget it,' he mumbled.

I put my arms around him. 'I've had a wonderful time, it was one of the best nights of my life, Zak.'

'Mine too,' he agreed, taking me in his arms and kissing me. We kissed for a long time and then, reluctantly, parted.

As dawn broke I lay awake, still wondering who Gloria was, and why Zak had been so quickly dismissive of her.

In the evenings I'd sit by the window with my sketchpad, thinking how lovely it would be to earn my living making hats and escape from the grind of the factory. I bought a yard of black felt in a fabric store on my way home one evening, and did my best to sew and shape it into a hat, the way Aunt Mabel had trained me. When Violet called round she seized it up at once. 'That's lovely, Ellie!' she said, holding it carefully, examining the tucks and decorative band.

'I thought I'd try something different,' I said, pleased with her response. 'Here, sit down, let me finish it off for you.' I continued cutting, folding, and pinning, turning it round and round so that I could judge it precisely, until what I'd imagined was before me. I dampened and steamed it into shape, then I trimmed it with a jet-black ribbon with the deft movements of my fingers. Its gleaming satin set off the hat. Violet's eyes followed the slow transformation of the plain shape into a proper hat. 'Try it on,' I said.

'It's lovely,' she said admiringly. 'You've certainly got talent.'

I told her of my plans to start up on my own soon. A plaintive note crept into my voice as I said, 'I should be going to dances, dating like the other girls, with my hair in a neat bob, and wearing silk stockings and smelling of eau de toilette, but I'm desperate to make my hats. It's a slow process, trying to save the money to get started, but I need a hat-shaper and some material to begin with.'

Violet said encouragingly, 'I could lend you the money to buy a hat-shaper – and we have an old sewing machine at home you could borrow, none of us uses it much. It works perfectly.'

'Oh Violet, that would be grand,' I said, choked. 'Are you sure?'

'Of course! Now dry your eyes and start sewing,' she said, her eyes twinkling.

I hugged her. 'You're a true friend.' I dabbed at my eyes with the back of my hand.

Later that week Violet delivered a little black sewing machine, in a wooden case with a handle, in her father's car.

'I'm going to buy some material to make hats in different kinds of fabrics and textures,' I told her.

'Let's go to Quincy market some day soon,' Violet said, 'you'll get bargains there.'

Shirlee didn't win the Seamstress of the Year competition. To my utter amazement and hers, I won it. When Mr Samuel presented me with the cheque, he made a little speech in which he predicted that I would go far in the trade and wished me well.

Afterwards, I said to Shirlee, 'I hope you don't mind my winning it.'

'Not at all.' She smiled. 'Ah'm after the big prize – Mr Samuel.'

Quincy market was packed with stalls of every kind, and full of Saturday-afternoon shoppers. Clothes hung from poles and awnings, stallholders shouted out their bargains to the jostling crowd. Boston housewives were busy buying everything for their week's groceries. The air was fragrant with the smell of baking at the cake stalls.

At a fabric stall, I purchased several yards of straw, felt, tulle, lace, and ribbons for trimmings, needles and various coloured threads. After a snack of coffee and muffins Violet and I went to see a Laurel and Hardy movie.

Very soon the hat-shaper was delivered. I moulded and trimmed a hat on it and sewed it up on the little machine. As soon as it was finished, it went off to one of Violet's friends.

Then, Shirlee asked me to make her a hat for her cousin Cindy's wedding. I used golden straw, so fine it seemed almost transparent. I dampened and steamed it into shape, holding the hot iron close to the brim, making sure not to touch the straw, the way Aunt Mabel had taught me. Carefully, I stitched it, then braided it with a blue ribbon and added a silk rose with intricate petals that I took from my own straw hat. As I sewed I thought of Alice. Did she think I'd abandoned her? I longed to write to her, but I didn't dare.

When I finally got to bed that night I prayed for Alice, and Mam, Lucy and little Matthew.

I overslept the following morning and was late for work. As I sneaked past Miss Flint's office, she came out. 'You're late,' she said.

'Sorry, I didn't hear my alarm clock,' I said, flushed.

'If it happens again I'll dock your wages.' Hard-eyed she watched me go to my machine.

Shirlee said, 'You sure look deadbeat.'

'I stayed up late to finish your hat,' I admitted.

'You did! I can't wait to see it.'

That evening, I made Shirlee close her eyes while I placed the hat on her head, and keep them closed as I tilted the brim a little to the right. Stepping back I said, 'Now, you can look.'

The delicate strands of the brim framed her face beautifully. The blue ribbon emphasised the colour of her eyes and complimented her flaxen hair.

'Wait 'til Mr Samuel sees me in this,' she said excitedly, pulling the brim down over one eye.

'Mr Samuel?'

Patting down the hair on either side of her hat she said, 'He's escorting me to the weddin'. I'll have my hair cut in a shingle and buy a fitted frock. I've seen a nice silk one with buttons all down the front.' She smiled at her reflection in the mirror. 'Ah'll have his eyes poppin' outta his head,' she laughed, her eyes full of mischief. 'Mrs Samuel Levin. Doesn't it have a nice ring to it?'

'Oh, Shirlee, I hope you won't be disappointed if he doesn't propose,' I said, fearful for her.

She winked at me. 'This littl' ol' hat is going to do the trick. How much do ay owe you for it?'

'No charge, you can advertise it for me,' I said, thinking of the important business contacts that Mr Samuel would be bound to have. I smiled at Shirlee. 'But do you like him . . . you know, in that way . . . ?' I asked her.

'Sure I do. He's cute, and the beauty of it is that as soon as we're wed I'll be able to get on with my own life while he's playin' golf, and fishin' and stuff.'

'You've got it all worked out.'

Her eyelids drooped a little as she said, 'Is that a bad thing, Ellie? I could help my momma out. She's got five kids at home to feed, and times are hard.'

'No, it is not, and I know you'd be a good wife to Mr Samuel, given the opportunity,' I said, meaning it.

'You bet I will.' Her eyes shone with merriment. I loved this good-natured, funny girl, who had chosen me as her friend and had taken me under her wing, and I'd no doubt in my mind that Mr Samuel would be under her spell before long.

Shirlee arranged for us all to go for a swim after work one scorching day. She brought an old swimming costume of hers for me to wear. It was too big for me and hung around me like a rag.

'Look at her!' Dora laughed, grabbing me, and holding me for the rest of the girls to see. Mortified, I turned away from her too quickly, and slipped on the rocks, twisting my ankle. A fierce pain shot through my foot as I hauled myself up, my ankle swelling up like a balloon.

'Oh lordy! What've you gone and done?' Shirlee said, putting her hand gently on my foot.

At her touch I let out a yelp.

'It's sprained,' she pronounced, insisting I bathe it in the sea to get the swelling down. She bound it tight with her headscarf.

With Shirlee's help I hobbled back to my apartment. As soon as we got there, I lay back on my bed to rest while she prepared a supper of fried eggs and beans. I thought, with dismay, that Zak would be back in Boston, and this sprained ankle meant I wouldn't be able to go out with him. When Violet called to see me I confided in her my disappointment.

'I was so looking forward to seeing Zak at the weekend,' I said glumly.

'I don't see why he can't visit you here,' she said.

'I don't want him to see this place.' I looked around the shabby room.

'Don't be silly, Zak won't mind,' she laughed.

On Saturday afternoon, to my surprise, Zak came to visit me. 'Violet told me that you'd sprained your ankle,' he said, his voice full of concern. He put down the large grocery bag he was carrying on the table and his eyes took in the shabby room – but I was too pleased to see him to be embarrassed by it.

He demanded to see my damaged ankle, which was by now swollen to twice its normal size and more painful than ever. 'You need to get that swelling down, and something for the pain. I'll be back shortly.' He left and returned with Aspirin and an ice pack from the bar on the corner.

Tenderly, he tied the ice pack around my ankle and poured me a glass of water to wash down the Aspirin. From the grocery bag he produced a pot of spaghetti bolognese, which he heated up on one of the gas rings. The rich aroma wafted out, making my mouth water. 'I didn't know you were such a good cook,' I said, impressed.

'It's the only dish I know how to make!' He presented me with a plate of food. I relished every mouthful, in spite of the pain. While he washed up and made coffee I lay back on my pillows, feeling as spoilt as a small child.

Afterwards he said gently, 'Ellie, this is not a suitable place for you to live.'

'It's all I can afford, Zak.'

'Violet'll be looking for an apartment soon. Why don't you two move in together?'

I shook my head. 'I couldn't afford to live in the areas Violet will be looking at.'

'I'll talk to her, see if we can come up with some arrangement . . .'

'No Zak, please don't do that. This apartment may not be much, but at least it's mine.'

He shrugged. 'If you insist.' He took me in his arms. 'I'll leave you to get some rest, Miss Independent. I'll be back tomorrow with some more groceries.'

'Honestly, you don't have to.'

'I want to,' he said, kissing me tenderly.

The following day the swelling had gone down quite a bit, and I felt well enough to sit at the window and watch for Zak's arrival. Sure enough, he came laden with parcels.

'I've brought lunch,' he said unpacking lobster, baked potatoes, and dressed salad from his favourite delicatessen. 'And pecan pie for afters!'

'I'll be as fat as a fool if I eat all of this. I exclaimed.

Zak laughed. 'More of you to love, then,' he said as he prepared our meal.

Afterwards he played some of our favourite Duke Ellington, Irving Berlin, and George Gershwin tunes on his portable wind-up gramophone. When he played '*Oh, Lady Be Good*' I melted into his arms, Gloria well and truly forgotten.

Fifteen

The following Saturday, Violet brought me a cutting of an advertisement in 'Positions Vacant' in the Boston Globe: *Milliner wanted immediately for exclusive shop in city centre. Very good wages.*

'That would be a post worth getting; a great opportunity for you,' Violet said, presenting me with a page of her house stationery with its embossed address and telephone number. I wasted no time in applying for the position.

A few days later she called to say that I was to phone a Miss Henderson about the job. Nervously, I made the call and was asked in for an interview. It was wonderful! I couldn't believe it, and stayed up late adding the finishing touches to my sample hats. I couldn't sleep with excitement.

On the day of my interview I walked to the subway with Violet, who had come along to give me support. We made our way to the small, exclusive store in Newbury Street. The shop was the essence of good taste, with pale green carpets, gold-coloured floor-length velvet curtains, the soft flattering glow of amber lamps.

The young girl behind the counter, with shining bobbed hair, and wearing a drop-waisted dress of rose silk, gave us a snooty look. 'Can I help you with something?' she asked coldly.

'I'm here to see Miss Henderson,' I said, confidently.

The girl said, with more than a hint of satisfaction, 'Miss Henderson might be a while, could you take a seat by the door, please?'

Nervously, I sat close to Violet on a row of seats just inside the door. While we waited she did her best to buoy me up. The full-length mirror in front of me assured me that my skirt and coat were at least respectable. The customers milling about looked to be well turned-out wealthy ladies. I noticed an elegant woman trying on a burgundy velvet hat, leaning towards the mirror, narrowing her eyes, then frowning with dismay at her reflection.

'Not quite what I'm looking for,' she said to the assistant, her disappointment obvious.

And you won't find it, I thought, because it isn't on the shelf . . . yet. The hat I would make for her would be out of this world. I envisioned a shooting feather to emphasise her strong cheekbones.

Finally Miss Henderson arrived. She was expensively dressed in a grey suit with frills and tucks on the bodice, and a grey helmet of a hat that looked more like a galvanised roof on her head and concealed the upper part of her face. Carefully removing it, she sat down on a chair behind the counter, fished her spectacles out of her lizard-skin bag, and putting them on looked at me with hard eyes. 'You must be Miss O'Rourke,' she said coolly.

My voice faltered just a little. 'I am . . . I'm here about the position you advertised . . .'

'Indeed,' she said calmly. 'Did you say you were a trained milliner?'

'Well, no . . . not yet,' I said, finding it difficult to keep my smile in place.

'Have you any kind of reference from a previous employer, then?'

'Well, not from a milliner,' I said honestly. 'I was trained by my aunt . . . who herself was trained by Jeffrey Rowe of New York.' I picked up my bag. 'These hats are samples of my work.'

She let out an impatient sigh as she took the bag. 'I think there has been a misunderstanding. I need a *trained* milliner and, preferably, a more . . . mature woman working for me. You would need to have at least three years of training and a qualification from one of the design houses before you would be considered by us.'

'But, I . . .' I began, close to tears.

Still holding out my bag, as if it contained rubbish, she stood up. My hands shook as I took it from her. She nodded curtly at me, as though I was dismissed, and picked up the telephone on her desk, just to emphasise that the conversation was closed.

I stood meekly, straightened my coat and adjusted my hat, and motioned to Violet, who stood too, gripping my hand. I walked outside, trembling, wondering if I'd ever again get an opportunity like the one I'd just missed.

'Honestly! How rude,' Violet exclaimed, linking her arm through mine.

'She's right, Violet,' I said. 'I won't get a job like that one without experience, and where am I going to get that?'

Violet's eyes flashed. 'You'll do it, I know you will. What was that fool of a woman thinking . . . not even looking at your hats!'

As we sat having coffee in a nearby café, Violet had an idea.

'I think perhaps you could make your appearance more interesting for the next interview,' she said. 'I can help you, if you want me to.'

'Really?' I asked, looking down at my clothes.

'Yes. You've a lovely figure, Ellie – and your clothes are decent – but perhaps you need to be more confident in your appearance. If you're perfectly groomed, you'll be more relaxed and charming, and you'll get away with anything. You'll see.'

Violet got to work that evening round at my place. She trimmed my eyebrows with tweezers and brushed them into shape, unpinned my hair and shook it out.

'I think you'd better bob your hair,' she said evenly. 'It's all the rage at the moment.'

'What?' I almost collapsed.

'If you want to work in the starry firmament of society milliners, you'll have to keep up with the fashions. Bobbed hair is a necessity. I think we'll pay a visit to the hairdresser.'

I faltered, but only for an instant. 'When?'

'No time like the present. I know a place. Come on!'

In the hairdresser's, my heart beat violently as I was seated on a high stool. The hairdresser, a pretty girl in a white coat, removed my tortoiseshell combs and began parting my hair slowly. For a second I almost cried out that it was a mistake, that I'd changed my mind. Then I closed my eyes, clenched my hands and sat perfectly still as the silver scissors snaked through my dark locks.

'There,' she said. I opened my eyes and flinched at the full extent of the damage that had been done. My hair lay in lank lifeless bangs on either side of my unrecognisable, pinched face. Far from looking like the charming and poised girl Violet had promised, I looked plain ridiculous. The hairdresser swung the mirror round to show me the back and there was an awkward pause.

'Don't you like it?' she asked, passing a comb through it, her eyes resting coldly on me before turning to

Violet. I glimpsed their exchange of glances before I burst into tears.

'I'm really sorry, I thought you'd love it,' Violet said, amazed at my reaction.

'It'll be all right . . . It's a bit of a shock,' I sniffed.

'Don't worry, I'll fix it so that it'll look slick.' She tossed her own hair to demonstrate how mine could look with careful grooming.

'Come on, we're going to splash out on an outfit for you,' she added, patting her purse.

'I can't take your money,' I said, overwhelmed.

'Nonsense! You can pay me back sometime if you feel that bad about it,' she said.

We went to Macy's, where we purchased a very expensive blue twill skirt and jacket in the latest style. The short jacket had tucks around the waist and the skirt was tapered and stopped at mid-calf. With a new, bright red lipstick and elegant shoes I finally looked a picture of competence and style. Violet fussed over my hair, which I was already getting used to, and suddenly, what had begun as a disastrous day, seemed one full of hope, after all. We laughed along the street, my inhibitions forgotten.

Zak loved my hair when we met that weekend. He decided that we should dine at Marco's, his favourite Italian restaurant, before going on to a nightclub. He took my arm as we went into the old restaurant, with its whitewashed walls and uneven floors. There were important Bostonians there: beautifully groomed and coiffed women in fine clothes, and important-looking men with self-satisfied expressions.

Zak explained some of the dishes and ordered for both of us. I felt perfectly content until I saw him staring at a table in the corner. I glanced towards the group of people sitting at it and then I looked back at Zak, who seemed tense. 'What's wrong?' I asked.

He lowered his voice. 'We can't stay here, we have to go,' he said, getting to his feet.

'But why?'

'I'll explain later,' he said urgently. He caught my arm as we stood up and hurried me out the door. Once out on the street he looked at me awkwardly. 'I didn't want them to see me,' he said feebly.

'Why? Do you owe them money or something?' I laughed.

'No, nothing like that. The man that was sitting in the corner is my father's best friend.'

I bristled. 'Am I of such low breeding that it would be belittling for you to have to introduce me to them?' Dare he not be seen in company with me? I thought.

'No! No it's nothing like that.' He put his arm around me. 'You've got it all wrong.'

I drew back quickly. 'I don't believe you.'

'It's true. It really has nothing to do with you.'

I turned to him. 'It has everything to do with me,' I said

furiously. 'If I'm not good enough to be introduced to your family friends, then I'm not good enough for you.' My voice was trembling, so were my hands. He swung away from me. My heart plunged as I went on, 'And there was I, thinking that you wanted to be with me.' I could hear distant laughter echoing in the icy darkness.

'No, no! That's not it.' Zak passed a hand over his brow. 'I do want to be with you, Ellie. More than anything in the world.' I noted the sad droop of his mouth and, for a second, I felt sorry for him.

'What is it then?'

'That man is president of our rival bank. I'm expected to marry his daughter.'

His words struck me like a blow in the face. Shocked, I was speechless, as he stood like a stranger looking down at me.

When I finally found my voice I said, 'Why didn't you tell me this before?'

'I was going to tell you.'

'When?'

'There never seemed a right time.'

'You're a liar. Pretending that I'm your girl when all the time you're planning to marry someone else. You make me sick.'

He caught up with me, walked alongside me, while I kept going.

'Wait, Ellie, let me explain. Gloria means nothing to me,' he shouted after me.

I wheeled around. 'Gloria!'

'Yes.' He passed a hand over his eyes as if he couldn't bear to look at me. 'Ellie, I don't want to marry her.'

'If you expect me to believe *that* then you're more pathetic that I thought.'

I walked away from him. His voice seemed to come from a great distance as he said, 'Ellie, wait!'

'I'm going home,' I said in a flat voice that I didn't recognise as my own.

'Ellie, don't let this come between us.' His voice held a pleading note as he came to me and took my hand. I snatched it away, and marched on.

He caught up with me, and grabbed my hand again. I broke free of him, and ran as fast as I could. This time he didn't follow me.

By the time I got back to my room, the blood seemed to have drained from my body. I crawled into bed, but I was too furious with Zak to sleep. The nerve of him letting me find out about his 'arranged marriage' in the most humiliating way possible. And why had Violet never mentioned it? If she'd known all along that there was no future for Zak and me, surely she could have said something, couldn't she? I felt confused.

My bell rang, making me jump sky-high.

'Who is it?' I called out when I got to the door.

'Ellie, It's Zak. I need to speak to you.'

'Go away.'

'Please,' he begged. 'Just open the door.'

179

I unlocked it, but left the chain on. 'What do you want?' I asked quietly.

'I need to explain,' he said.

'Save it for some other mug. I'm not listening.' I slammed the door in his face, went back to bed, and burst into tears. Nothing would convince me that I wasn't just a silly romantic fool he'd met on-board ship. I'd known all along that he was out of my league, but I'd denied it to myself and let things go on.

That night I dreamed that I was at home, standing in my bare feet in the sea, waiting for Dad. When I saw him in the distance, floating among the rocks, I cried out to him that I was here to help him, but my voice wouldn't carry above the crashing waves. I shouted and shouted as I saw him sinking deeper and deeper into the sea, but only a whining sound came out. I waded into the sea after him, screaming, 'Dad! Don't go, Dad. Wait, I'll help you!'

I woke up with a start. It was morning.

In a daze, and weak from a sleepless night I dragged myself out of bed, exhausted. The more I tried not to think about Zak during the morning, the more thoughts of him crowded in. I tried to convince myself that I was better off without him, at the same time wondering if I was making the biggest mistake of my life by not listening to his explanation.

'Hey, what's up, Ellie? Why're ya slumped over your

sewing machine – are ya sick or somethin'?' Shirlee asked, concerned. I told her what had happened, unable to keep it to myself a minute longer. 'He made a fool of me. I was stupid to consider him a boyfriend.'

'But that's what he is.'

'No, he pretended to be. He took advantage of me,' I heard myself say.

Shirlee clicked her tongue. 'Surely Violet would have told ya about that girl if there'd been somethin' to it.'

'Maybe Violet didn't know anything about it.'

'Don't you think she'd have spotted them together sometime if he'd been seein' her?'

'I suppose so,' I said begrudgingly, still wanting to believe the best of Zak.

'You need to talk to him, find out.'

That evening I waited by my window watching the distant wavering lights of the harbour, listening to the tuneless tinkling of piano keys floating up from downstairs, hoping that Zak would come to see me. When there was no sign of him, I went to see Violet.

'This is a pleasant surprise,' she said with a warm smile as she opened the door.

'Violet, why didn't you tell me that Zak is spoken for?' I burst out.

She looked at me, perplexed. 'What do you mean, spoken for?'

'He's going to marry Gloria.'

'Gloria!'

'Yes, according to him there's been an arrangement between both their families for years. Didn't you know?'

Violet looked totally perplexed, 'I've met Gloria several times, and it has never struck me that she and Zak are anything but friends. Certainly nothing was ever said to me about it. Are you absolutely sure?'

'Yes.' Tearfully, I told her what had happened at the restaurant. 'Gloria's the bride they've set their hearts on for him because her daddy's president of a bank. It makes sense; think of the future they'll all have with a merger like that,' I said bitterly.

Violet shook her head in disbelief. 'I'll go ask Aunt Anita, she'll tell me the truth.'

Sixteen

Shirlee hadn't returned from her cousin's wedding. When Mr Samuel, looking very smart in a black fancy-cut coat, a high-collared shirt, and a white silk cravat, asked me to step into his office one morning, I was certain that he was going to tell me that something awful had happened to her.

'Is it Shirlee? Is she OK?'

'She's fine,' he smiled reassuringly. 'I told her to stay and have a little break with her family. She'll be back soon. Sit down, Miss O'Rourke, I want a word with you.' He pointed to a chair and took a seat behind his desk.

'Yes?' I held my breath.

'Yours are the nicest hats I've seen in a long time . . .' he began.

'Oh, thank you,' I blushed.

He leaned towards me. 'Shirlee tells me you're anxious to set yourself up as a milliner one day.'

'That's what I'm aiming for, Mr Samuel.'

He leaned forward. 'I know this milliner guy, a Mr Duchamp. He has a small, exclusive place off Clarendon

Street. He's looking for an apprentice. I told him I got a girl on my factory floor that makes fancy hats but needs training. He said he'd be interested in seeing you.'

'He did!'

He lit a cigar, puffed out the smoke. 'Of course, I'd be sorry to lose you but I hate to see talent go to waste. Anyone can sew straight seams. Hats, now that's a different matter. Would you like me to fix you up with an interview?'

'An interview! Oh Mr Samuel! I don't know what to say.'

He smiled, and said in a confidential tone, 'I'd be grateful if you wouldn't mention it to the other girls.'

'Not even to Shirlee?'

'Especially not to Shirlee. She'd only be disappointed if nothing comes of it.'

'OK, and thank you, Mr Samuel. I'm really grateful to you.'

'Anyone'd do the same.' He stood up, went to the door and opened it. 'I'll phone Mr Duchamp right away. I'm sure he'll want to see you real soon.' The eagerness in his eyes never wavered as I left his office.

I found it difficult to keep my mind on my work for the rest of the day, so great was my excitement. I couldn't wait to see Violet to tell her. Also, I was dying to know if she'd found out anything about Zak and that Gloria. So, after work, I went to see her and told her my great news.

'Oh, Ellie, I'm thrilled for you,' she cried, giving me a bear hug.

'Thanks, I can't believe it myself. Did you find out anything about Zak?' I asked, dying to know but also scared of hearing what she might tell me.

She gave me a sympathetic look. 'Aunt Anita did say that she and Uncle Henry have been hoping and praying for a marriage between Zak and Gloria ever since they were children.' Seeing my expression, she said hastily, 'That's not to say it'll happen. He really likes you, Ellie. I know he does.'

'For a bit of fun, nothing serious.'

'That's not true.'

I sighed. 'What difference will it make? His parents will probably get their way.'

She frowned. 'I agree that they're a big influence on him where his job is concerned, but I doubt that he'll let them dictate who he should marry.'

'I'm not convinced of that,' I said sadly.

Mr Samuel made an appointment for me to see Mr Duchamp on the following Monday afternoon. The tiny, cobbled lane off Clarendon Street was hot and quiet. I stopped at a sign above a door that read: *Duchamp – Haute Couture Designs Made to Measure*.

I stood under the awning, gazing in through the window at the magnificent silk evening hats, with soft, caressing folds and veils, glad of the shade to powder my nose and fix the new brilliant feather in my hat, my heart beating wildly. Squaring my shoulders, I pressed a button marked 'Bell'. It tinkled, and a tall, elegant woman in a black dress opened the door.

'May I help you?' she asked stiffly.

'My name is Eleanor O'Rourke. I have an appointment to see Mr Duchamp,' I told her.

'Come in – just a moment,' she said, and went upstairs. While she was gone I looked at the bolts of various types of material, in the most beautiful colours, packed neatly on shelves. Gloves, fur collars and cuffs, and belts were displayed neatly on the counter.

'Mr Duchamp will see you now,' she said when she returned. 'Upstairs – first on your left.'

I went up the stairs to a door marked 'PRIVATE' and knocked. The door was opened immediately and I almost collided with a tall, distinguished-looking man in a well-cut suit. His black hair shone, his teeth flashed.

'Miss O'Rourke! Good to meet ya.' He looked me up and down with a fastidious expression.

I cleared my throat and said, 'How do you do, Mr Duchamp.'

His face glowed with good humour as we shook hands. With a flash of his gold ring he gestured for me to take a seat. I could almost hear my knees knocking together with fear as I sat down opposite him.

'Mr Samuel tells me that you want to be a milliner,' he said, raising his eyebrows.

'Yes, I do.'

'And tell me, have you any experience at all?'

Determined not to make the same mistake I had made at the previous interview, I said without hesitation, 'I learned how to make hats with my Aunt Mabel, who trained with the top milliner, Jeffrey Rowe, in New York. She runs her own successful business in Ireland. She taught me a great deal about millinery.'

He looked at me in an intent way, then leaned back in his chair. 'And you want to serve your apprenticeship?'

'Yes, I do. I've brought along some samples of my designs,' I said handing my bag to him.

'So, what have we got here?' he asked with a condescending laugh, peeping inside, then taking each hat out carefully, and examining it. He looked impressed.

'You are a talented girl, Miss O'Rourke. I can see your potential in these hats.'

'Thank you, Mr Duchamp.'

His clear brown eyes considered me gravely. 'We make hats for Boston ladies who are looking for something . . . a little more stylish than the standard type hat. They want hats that will make them look beautiful. Of course,' he went on, 'there are many factors involved when designing a hat. We take our client's personality, colouring, skin tone, body shape, and hair length into consideration.' His smile faltered a little as he went on, 'I could give you an apprenticeship, but it would be a trial period and the salary I could offer would only be ten dollars a week. What do you think?'

'I think it would be a wonderful opportunity for me, Mr Duchamp,' I blurted out, disgracing myself, babbling on about how much I appreciated his kindness and how I'd make sure that he wouldn't regret his decision. 'I can't thank you enough,' I said, breathless.

His smile was back in place. 'I admire your courage, Miss O'Rourke.' He looked at me curiously. 'My mother was Irish. She was a hard worker. It's a cultural trait. She too had it hard when she first came to New York . . . Tell me, are you from a large family?'

'I'm one of five children. My mother is a widow.'

'I'm sorry to hear that,' he said kindly. 'You must miss home, but you're doing fine from what I can see!' He glanced at his watch, and got to his feet. 'Now, when can you start?'

'I'll have to serve a week's notice at the factory.'

'We'll see you Monday week then, nine o'clock sharp.'

'Yes, Mr Duchamp. Thank you.'

With a sweep of his hand he escorted me to the door. 'Goodbye Miss O'Rourke,' he said with a ravishing smile.

When I saw Shirlee at her bench next morning, I rushed ahead with my good news without thinking to ask her how she was.

'That's wonderful,' she said enthusiastically. 'But I'm sure goin' to miss you when you're gone.'

'We'll meet up in the evenings, catch up on all the gossip.'

She sighed. 'It won't be the same. Still, I don't think I'll be here much longer maself.'

'Why? Did Mr Samuel propose?'

She dropped her voice. 'Not yet, but I hope and pray he's gonna do it soon because . . . well . . . between you and me I think I'm pregnant.'

'Shirlee! Are you sure?'

'Shh . . . keep your voice down. Yes, I'm sure,' she sighed, placing her hand protectively across her tummy. 'Ay wasn't going to tell anyone but I'm goin' outta my mind with worry.'

'Oh Shirlee! I don't know what to say.'

She sat back. 'Don't say nothin'.' She blinked back the tears.

'Have you told Mr Samuel yet?'

She shook her head. 'I don't have the courage. I'm scared that I've gone and ruined everythin'.'

I put my arm around her shoulders. 'I'm sure you won't have,' I said, trying to sound convincing. 'But I do think you should talk to him soon.'

'I will. Listen to me goin' on about maself, and I never thought to ask you about Zak. Have ya heard from him?'

'No, not a word.'

'Still pinin' for him?' She looked at me.

'Yes, but for the Zak that I used to know. Not the one he turned out to be.'

She smiled. 'He's still the same person he always was, Ellie. He's good lookin' and funny, and he makes your heart race.'

'Yes he does,' I agreed, and as I sat sewing for the rest of the day I thought of him. How he used to call me his 'Irish colleen', and laughingly mimic my brogue, and how he'd hold me close to him and kiss me tenderly. I did know him. I knew him well enough to love him.

'And while ya worryin' about whether you know him or not, that Gloria will snatch him from you. Are they engaged? Is she wearing his ring?'

'His ring!' A shiver of fear ran down my spine that almost knocked the breath out of me at the very thought of it.

Shirlee gave me a steely look. 'Ellie, don't be a fool. Stop lookin' over your shoulder all of the time and fearin' every girl that crosses his path.'

'I never did until now.'

'Well, don't leave it until it's too late to do something about it. See him and have it out. Promise me?' She caught my wrist and held it until I made that promise then, with a twinkle in her eyes, she said, 'I'll dance at your wedding.'

'I'll dance at yours first.'

'I sure hope so,' she said doubtfully.

Seventeen

On a hot Monday morning, I started my apprenticeship at Duchamp's workshop in a back lane off Newbury Street. My heart was pounding and my throat was dry with nervousness as I walked into the busy workroom, where three women were working at cluttered workbenches.

A thin woman with slightly stooped shoulders introduced herself as Miss Sweet, the head milliner. She led me to a workbench and handed me a shaper. Pointing to a basket of fabrics in the corner, she said, 'Take one of those cut-offs and let me see what you can do.'

Under her watchful eye I was all fingers and thumbs as I tried to shape a hat. Exasperated, she took the fabric from me saying, 'You've picked up some bad habits along the way. Here, let me show you. Always cut the fabric on the shaper; never lay it down to cut it. Now, have a go.' I tried to do it her way and couldn't. Frustrated she said, 'I reckon a monkey could make a better job of it than you're doing.' She demonstrated it again. 'Keep trying,' she said and left me to it.

One of the other women said under her breath, 'You'll get used to her giving you orders.'

'I'm nervous,' I confessed to her.

'It's your first day, you'll get the hang of it,' she smiled.

The girl next to me, about my age, said, 'I'm Gracie, watch what I do.'

I copied what she was doing and by the time Miss Sweet returned to examine my work I had it right. There was no praise from her, just a nod to continue on.

By the end of the day every muscle in my body ached. On the way out, Miss Sweet called me over. 'Your shaping is better than it was this morning. I'll keep my eye on you for the next few days, see how you're doin'.' Her eyes were steely.

'Yes Miss Sweet.' I left, shaking from head to toe.

But the following day Miss Sweet seemed pleased with my progress. 'Now thread up that sewing machine and start stitching it all together.'

Under the sharp white teeth of the unfamiliar sewing machine, the threads twisted into a zigzag. Miss Sweet said crossly, 'This is basic stuff, you should be able to do it blindfold. Start again.'

I practised all day. 'That's better, keep going,' she said, when she saw my finished work. I rubbed my aching thumbs and wrists and began again.

★ ★ ★

One morning I was surprised to glance up and see Mr Duchamp standing beside me, watching me work. 'How are you getting along, Ellie?' he asked.

'OK thanks, Mr Duchamp,' I smiled.

'Good.' With a nod and a smile he left. I followed his retreating figure with my eyes, only to find Miss Sweet standing over me, her face puce with rage.

'Watch what you're doing,' she cried. I looked down and saw to my horror that a thread had caught in the sewing machine and was running the length of the fabric. 'Mr Duchamp thinks you're a find but I have my doubts about you. I'll have to complain about you to him if you make any more mistakes.' My heart sank. Only just a week in the place and I was about to be fired.

'What's going on?' Neither of us had seen Mr Duchamp standing there.

'I snagged a thread and ruined a piece of fabric.' Mortified, I removed it from under the shuttle and held it out for him to see.

'She's a bit careless,' Miss Sweet said.

For a moment his face looked stern, then he said, 'I'm sure you're willing to overlook it this time, Miss Sweet. It's all new to Eleanor, give her a chance.' He looked at her questioningly. Red-faced, she had no choice but to agree.

I kept my eyes on the intricacies of the stitches from then on, my feet moving steadily on the treadle as I slowed down. Carefully, I removed the material from under the metal foot, snipped off the thread, then threaded the needle with different coloured thread and started another line, until the lines of stitching were as delicate as a spider's web.

As soon as I'd mastered the sewing I worked separately on crowns and brims. Miss Sweet, for all her impatience, was a good teacher. She drew pictures of the type of hats she wanted us to make, explaining the importance of the silhouette, lines, and shapes.

I learned how to insert wire into brims, how to make china silk, and Georgette and velvet roses for the trims. I even learned how to dye colours to get the special 'Duchamp' shade.

As part of our training Miss Sweet took us to the wholesale millinery supply stores, where she taught us how to select feathers, flowers and trimmings for each different type of hat. She explained the difference between good material and the cheap kind, and showed me how to tell a good ribbon from an imitation one. She knew the true art of millinery, and I admired her for the high standards she demanded from us.

Shirlee called at my apartment one evening to see me and I was shocked by her downcast appearance. Her hair was lacklustre and her cheeks were sunken.

'Have you spoken to Mr Samuel yet?' I asked her.

She shook her head. 'I'm waitin' for the right

moment,' she said sheepishly. I could tell that the anxiety of it all was becoming too much for her.

'I don't think you should keep it to yourself much longer, Shirlee. Mr Samuel needs to know so that he can look after you.'

'I'll tell him. I'm not sure how he'll take it.'

'He'll be thrilled,' I assured her, hoping I was right.

One morning, about a month later, Mr Duchamp sent for me.

'Miss Baker's busy in the store,' he said. She needs an assistant. You'd be ideal for the job, and you could continue with the hats in the workroom when it's quiet. Of course there'd be a little more cash in your wage packet. How would that suit you?'

I jumped at the opportunity, and started in the shop the following morning.

'I hope you're tidy. Everything has to be kept it its proper place,' Miss Baker said, indicating the neat spools of ribbons and labelled boxes of trimmings.

The bell tinkled. A rich-looking lady came in. Miss Baker greeted her like an old friend and introduced me to her as her new assistant. The lady ordered a cocktail hat for the Yacht Club ball. Miss Baker circled her head with a tape measure, jotted down the measurement in a large order book, then she produced some sample hats, pointed at one, saying, 'What about something like this?' It was a velvet petal cocktail cloche.

'Oh, that one would be wonderful,' the lady said, delighted.

Miss Baker wrote down the code number of the design and details of the material in her book. 'Would you like us to make you a hat to match another of your outfits, madam?'

'Perhaps, I'll let you know,' the lady said and left.

As soon as she was gone Miss Baker said to me, 'You can start on that hat this afternoon if we're not busy.'

Under Miss Sweet's guidance I made the hat to the delight of our customer. For my next creation I was allowed to make a hat for a bride's honeymoon. I trimmed the brim to suit the shape of her face, and added flowers to match and veiling as fine as spun sugar. Miss Baker liked the dainty hat so much that she placed it on a stand in the window, and arranged a matching cape and gloves beneath it. The display looked just like the ones in those elegant windows I'd admired on Fifth Avenue.

Women passing by paused to take delight in the display. When our client returned, she was enchanted with her new hat. Her bridesmaid came in next day and ordered a bleached straw cloche trimmed with a lilac taffeta ribbon.

From then on, I was in the workroom making the hats to order more often than I was in the shop. I made a child's blue satin cloche for a birthday party, a lilac sequinned one, and an ivory straw cloche for a wedding.

On my way home one evening I bought a copy of *Vogue*, the new haute couture magazine from Paris, to check their latest millinery styles.

Miss Sweet was enchanted with the crochet and chenille hats in the new coral shade when I showed them to her, and suggested that we experiment with them. She taught us how to make them, only hers were more elaborate than anything that had been seen before, and the colours were more daring. And we used the neatest of hand-stitches to tuck and embroider. Every scrap of ribbon and fold of fabric that we used was accounted for in Miss Baker's leather-bound ledger.

The word spread. Our hats were ordered for all occasions: dances, cocktail parties, weddings, christenings, even for outings in the houses of the wealthy. We worked from early morning until late at night fulfilling the demands. When a delighted Mr Duchamp gave me a raise at the end of six months, I was so thrilled that I sent Alice five dollars with a little note telling her to buy herself a treat, though I made sure not to put my address on the note.

On the following Sunday, Violet and I went to the cinema to see Clara Bow and Glen Hunter in the movie, *Grit*. Then we ate at a doughnut bar that sold a whole variety: chocolate, sugared, cinnamon, everything you could think of.

'There's a special jazz orchestra from Chicago playing at a dance at the Fairmont hotel tonight,' Violet said excitedly. 'Would you like to come?'

'I'd love to,' I said, pleased to have something to look forward to.

The lights from tall buildings burned brightly as we followed girls in flowing skirts with velvet hats and matching capes through the revolving doors into the swarming gold and marble lobby of the Fairmont hotel.

The ballroom was vast. Spotlights on the ceiling threw flickering colours over the long swishing gowns of the dancing ladies, giving them a glittering, magical quality. Violet and I danced our hearts out, changing partners with every tune. I was doing the Charleston, swinging my elbows, stamping my feet to the double beat of the drums when I turned suddenly and came face to face with Zak.

'Ellie!' His hand closed over mine. 'You're looking very pretty,' he said.

It took all the courage that I could muster to meet his gaze. He looked so handsome, in a black suit and dazzling white shirt. 'You're looking very well too. I didn't expect to see you here,' I said, flustered, looking around frantically for Violet to rescue me.

'I'm back in Boston now. I'm working in a brokerage house, selling bonds.' Drawing me to one side he said, 'How are you?'

'I'm very well, thank you.'

As we stood there, the past drifted back. I wanted him to take me in his arms and hold me close but suddenly I caught sight of Gloria, her face dark with annoyance.

'I think your friend is waiting for you,' I said sharply.

All at once she was beside us. 'There you are, Zak. You came here with me, remember?' she drawled sweetly.

'I just bumped into Ellie. We've been catching up. Gloria, you remember Eleanor O'Rourke?'

'Gloria, nice to see you again,' I said, extending my hand, forcing myself to be polite.

'Likewise,' she said, shaking it, her voice dripping with insincerity.

As the music started up again Gloria turned to Zak. 'I don't want to miss the next dance,' she said, crushing me with a look that made it obvious that it was time for me to make myself scarce.

Turning to the nice-looking man next to me, I took his arm and said, 'I promised you this next one, didn't I?' and moved off with my astonished partner.

Behind me I heard Gloria's sharp burst of 'Oh sure' as she marched off.

After the dance I thanked my bewildered partner and went to look for Violet. 'Zak's here.'

'I know.' She blushed.

Annoyed with her, I said, 'So you were hoping to do a bit of matchmaking again?'

'No, I just wanted to get you two talking, that's all.'

'Gloria's with him.'

'I didn't know she'd be here. Sorry.'

'Well, I'm going, I don't want to bump into them again.'

'Wait, I'll come with you.'

'No, you stay and enjoy yourself. I'll get a cab on the corner.' And I was gone before she could argue with me.

Outside, the street was dark and deserted. Pulling my coat on, I walked quickly towards the taxi rank.

'Ellie!'

I turned to see Zak approaching me. I stood uncertain as to what to do.

'You shouldn't be out here alone like this,' he said.

'I'm getting a cab.' I began walking.

'Wait, Ellie. I'm sorry about what happened earlier – with Gloria.'

'Where is she?' I asked, looking around, pretending that I hadn't seen her storm off earlier.

'She went home,' he said, unruffled. 'Listen, I'd like to talk to you, properly.'

'I don't think so.'

'Ellie, Gloria's just a friend.'

'Do you honestly expect me to believe that, if you can keep something as important as a marriage arrangement to yourself for so long? I just wonder what else there is you're not telling me.'

'But that's the point, Ellie. Gloria's not my girlfriend, and she never will be. She's like a sister to me.'

'I don't think *she* sees it that way.'

Zak blushed. 'That's up to her.'

I started walking towards the corner. There were no cabs at the rank. 'This is silly, let me take you home,' Zak said.

'I don't seem to have a choice.'

As we drove along he said, 'Violet told me about your apprenticeship. She says you're makin' swell hats.'

I relaxed a little. 'Yes, I'm training in Duchamp and loving every minute of it,' I said. 'And what about your new job?'

'I'm dealing in some good stocks,' Zak looked out of the window. 'And it's great to be back in Boston . . . Near you.' There was a silence as I tried not to feel pleased at his words, and then as he pulled up outside my apartment he turned to me suddenly. 'What about lunch tomorrow, for old time's sake?'

I didn't have the willpower to resist him. 'All right, then,' I said.

'Good. I'll pick you up at twelve-thirty. No, make that twelve.'

Zak took me to a restaurant near the harbour. Over a delicious meal of tortellini and a bottle of red wine, he told me how much he liked being back in Boston and all about his new job. 'I should be a wizard with the markets soon,' he said enthusiastically. 'And you'll be a wizard with your hats?' he added, and I couldn't help but smile. I told him more about Duchamp, and my latest creations. He seemed genuinely pleased for me. We chatted about Violet and her family, then Zak said, 'Friends of mine are having a party tonight, will you come with me?'

'I hesitated. That would be nice. But I can't stay out too late. I start work at eight o'clock.'

'I'll have you home early, I promise,' he assured me.

At the party, Zak introduced me to his friends Fred and Floyd, and a girl called Nancy who stared at me and said, 'So, have you known Zak long?'

'I met him on the ship on the way here,' I told her.

'How cute,' she said.

The girls all seemed to shine with good grooming. Their clothes were the very best, their jewellery expensive. They reminded me of the rich girls I'd met on the ship.

When the conversation was of holidays and houses, swimming-pools and boats, I felt uncomfortable and out of place. Zak didn't seem to notice. He was enjoying himself too much, but I wasn't sure if I wanted to put myself through an ordeal like that again.

'Take no notice of them,' Shirlee said, when she came to see me and I told her about the party. 'Act like you're as good as they are. That's what I do with Mr Samuel's friends.'

'Have you talked to Mr Samuel yet?' I asked.

She shook her head, looking down at her now quite plump tummy. 'But I reckon I'd better tell him before he tells me.'

Eighteen

I was sitting by the window in my apartment, late one Saturday evening, busy stitching curved lines on a brim of a cloche hat for a friend of Violet's. The light was failing, but I had to take my time. Cutting corners with this kind of intricate work wouldn't do. Duchamp's reputation was at stake, and so was mine. One day, before too long, I hoped to see my hats on display in my own little store, being admired and bought by lots of wealthy ladies.

There was a knock on the door.

'Coming,' I called out, rubbing my eyes as I went to open the door, expecting to see Violet or Shirlee standing there.

'Uncle Jack!' My heart went crashing through my ribcage.

'Hello Ellie.' In his grey trilby hat, his black coat and black turtleneck sweater, he seemed like someone from another world – 'I've tracked you down at last,' he said, stepping past me into the room, gazing around for what seemed like an eternity.

I couldn't take it in. 'How did you know where to find me?'

His eyelids flickered. 'You mentioned the friends you made on the boat over, remember? I figured that you might come to Boston. Then the postmark on your letter to Alice confirmed it.' Seating himself down he said, 'You shouldn't have run away like that, Ellie. It was crazy. Anything could have happened to you.'

Anger and resentment bubbled up inside me. 'I'm safer here than I was in your house,' I said.

His face softened slightly. 'Well, I blame myself partly for letting Sally take control of you. It taught me a lesson I'll never forget. You won't have to work so hard like that again, I promise, and you can go to college.'

Astonished, I looked at him. 'I'm not going back, Uncle Jack. I'm doing all right here. I've got an apprenticeship. The people I work for are dependent on me. I can't leave them in the lurch.'

'Send them a note,' he smiled. 'They'll have no problem finding someone to replace you. Now go and pack up your things.'

'I'm not going with you.'

'Yes you are. Alice is pining for you, and your mam is out of her mind with worry over you,' he said.

'Tell Alice I'm sorry, but my life is here now. I'll write to Mam.'

He stood up. 'I'm here to take you back. I've got your

train ticket. The cab's waiting outside. Now get your things together, and come on.'

I faced him stubbornly. 'I'm not going back there. Never!'

He grabbed my arm. 'You're coming with me, *now*,' he said firmly. 'Go pack your suitcase, and hurry up.'

I stared at him, hardly believing what I was hearing.

'Are you deaf?' He came to me, lifted a hand as though to hit me, then corrected himself, and dropped it. 'Listen, I sponsored you to come to the States. You're a minor and I'm your legal guardian. You'll do as I say or I'll report you to the authorities. You know what they'll do? They'll throw you into a detention centre. You don't want that now, do you?' His eyes on me were dark and threatening.

A spurt of fear rose up in me. Panic-stricken, hardly believing what was happening, I went to my chest of drawers and threw a few things into a grip bag while he paced up and down agitatedly.

'Ready?' he asked.

'Yes,' I said, a hollow, empty feeling in the pit of my stomach.

'Right.' He was going through my sheaf of patterns.

'What are you doing?' I snapped.

'You'll need these.' He stuffed them into his coat pocket. 'Come on,' he commanded.

Before I could look around to see if there anything else that I could take with me, he pushed me through the door, down the stairs and out on to the road where the taxi was waiting. I stood stubbornly at the side of the road.

'Get in.' He gave me a shove, leaving me no choice.

The train station was crowded. Hordes of people with luggage were milling around. With his hand on the collar of my jacket, Uncle Jack walked me down the platform like a dog on a lead to where the New York bound train was waiting.

As he propelled me on to the train I turned to him. 'I'm not going,' I said, defiantly.

He seized my arm. 'You're coming with me if I have to carry you all the way,' he said through clenched teeth.

I tried to pull away from him but he only tightened his grasp. 'Stop making a scene,' he said, pushing me down the corridor. I jerked my arm away but he grabbed it again.

'I hate you!' I said through clenched teeth just as the engine of the train roared into life and drowned out my voice. Passengers stared as Uncle Jack pushed me roughly into a compartment that was filling up.

The whistle blew, the train accelerated. As we pulled out of Boston I cowered resentfully in the corner, my eyes on the grey metallic lines of track, the train swaying from side to side as we travelled through the twilight. Opposite me Uncle Jack stared out the window triumphantly, then nodded off. Soon he was fast asleep.

When the train rumbled into the first station, I got to my feet and silently backed out of the door of the compartment, then ran down the corridor just as it came to a halt. Pushing down on the handle of the door, I jumped down on to the platform, hitting it with a thump, and raced down the length of it.

'Stop that girl!' With a hammering heart, I heard Uncle Jack's voice, muffled by the noise of the train.

I pushed through a crowd coming towards me, rounded the corner and dived down a flight of steps and into another platform, where I mingled with people from another train as they headed towards the exit.

A ticket collector was standing at the gate. 'Ticket please,' he said pleasantly. I pretended to search the pockets of my coat while the ticket collector waited.

'I must have dropped it, I'll have a look. Back in a minute,' I said, and retraced my steps as casually as I could manage, pretending to search the ground as I went.

I could hear the train start up again, and the whistle blow, then everything went quiet.

I ran back to an empty platform on the far side of the tracks, and crossed a bridge that led out on to a dim-lit street. I'd gone some distance along the deserted road when I heard a voice like the crack of a whip call, 'Ellie!'

I turned around to see a big cop coming towards me, followed by Uncle Jack. With a burst of energy I scurried into a field and ran like the wind. Ahead of me I saw a gleam of silver, like a sword, and the green lights of the signal box that we'd passed on our way into the station. I reckoned that if I followed the train tracks I would find my way back to Boston.

I groped my way along the siding with nothing but black space all around me, only the track to guide me. As my eyes grew accustomed to the dark I could make out trees and hedges here and there, and realised that I was in open countryside. The wind rose and vibrated eerily through the tracks. An owl hooted, making me jump. I kept going.

I must have walked a couple of miles when I heard the far-off siren of a train. I turned to see two beams of light on a huge black train coming towards me. Scrambling up the bank, I hid my head in my drawn-up knees as it roared past, its wheels crackling off the tracks. Trembling, I looked down to see plumes of smoke rising like waves on either side of it as it thundered on, blowing hot air all around. It swung off into the distance, leaving a trail of blue smoke in its wake that made my eyes burn.

When the bank narrowed, I walked on a plank of track. The wind blew hard against my face and my knees ached. But I kept going.

As dawn broke, the sky grew pale and the sun appeared in the east, a golden globe with layers of Boston rooftops stacked up behind it. Then I saw the gleam of the Charles River and heard the muffled horns of the boats. I was almost there.

Once I neared the train station I walked past empty warehouses, stores and timber yards to Violet's home, my legs so tired that I could barely drag myself along. When I reached her apartment, she opened the door almost as soon as I rang the bell.

'Ellie!' she cried, shocked, leading me inside. 'Look at the state of you, what's happened?'

'Uncle Jack came and . . .' I broke down.

'Here, come and sit down.' Gently she removed my ruined shoes and, over a cup of hot, strong coffee and a buttered muffin, I told her the whole story. 'I'm never going back to New York, Violet,' I sobbed, 'but I can't stay here in Boston. Oh, why had he to come here and spoil everything!' I burst into a bout of fresh tears.

'Sshh. You stay here, have a nice hot bath and a rest. I'll phone Zak as soon as I get into work. He'll know what to do.'

As soon as she left I took a long bath, let the hot water seep into my bones, then I dressed in some clean clothes that Violet had left out for me, and washed mine in her washtub. Afterwards, as I lay on the sofa waiting for Zak, I thought of the night I'd just been through. It all felt so strange, as if I'd had a dream and couldn't wake up from it.

Zak arrived soon after that. 'Ellie! Are you all right?' he asked, full of concern for me and outraged at what Uncle Jack had done.

'He says he's got rights over me, Zak,' I explained.

211

'He'll come back again, he won't give up. I'll have to go away,' I sobbed.

Zak pulled me close to him.

'Sshh . . . I have an idea. We have a summerhouse in Hyannis Port. I'll take you there. You'll be safe until we figure out what to do,' he said decisively.

'What about work and Mr Duchamp's urgent orders? I can't let our clients down.'

'I'll phone Mr Duchamp, say you're ill. He'll understand and I'm sure the other girls will cover for you. Now quit worrying.' Picking up the phone, he dialled a number. 'Hi Mrs Savino. It's Zak,' he said into the receiver. 'I'm coming down this afternoon with a friend. Will you make up my bed, and the one in the guest bedroom, and get in some fresh supplies, please . . . Sure . . . Thanks so much . . . See you later . . . Bye.' He replaced the receiver and turned back to me. 'Mrs Savino is our housekeeper at Hyannis Port – she lives next door to the summerhouse,' he explained. 'Don't worry, Ellie, you're safe now.'

Nineteen

We drove through beautiful wooded countryside and arrived at the Rubens' summerhouse late that afternoon. It was a white clapboard house, with big windows overlooking the bay, and a neat lawn surrounded by a white picket fence. Inside it was light and airy, and tastefully furnished with leather sofas and armchairs to match, and big, bright paintings of local scenes on the walls. In the kitchen a tall fridge was stocked with food and drink, waiting for the arrival of an army.

Zak led the way upstairs to a bedroom overlooking the bay. 'This is your room. Comfortable eh?' he said.

'It's gorgeous!' I exclaimed, gazing out at the sea.

'You take your time unpacking. Come on down when you're ready.'

'Thanks Zak,' I said gratefully, and after he'd left the room I went to the window to look at the view.

Sailing boats floated lazily on the bluest water I'd ever seen. People walked leisurely along the shore. It was paradise. I had a quick wash, dressed, and went downstairs.

Zak was brewing coffee. 'Mrs Savino left us steaks for supper. That OK with you?'

'Wonderful,' I said, hardly believing my good fortune.

Afterwards, we went for a walk along the strip of beach in the twilight, Zak telling about his boyhood summer holidays spent sailing and snorkelling with his cousins. The early moon shone on the sand and silvered the lapping waves. 'It's so beautiful, if I lived here I'd never want to leave it,' I said.

Zak smiled. 'I'd love to stay on, but I've got to go back to work in the morning,' he said. 'Mrs Savino'll be here first thing so you've no need to worry. Anything you want, she'll get it for you.'

'I can't thank you enough, Zak,' I said.

'I'm glad to be of help.' He kissed me so tenderly that I forgot about everything but him and the moment.

Next morning when I heard Zak getting ready to leave, I dressed quickly and went downstairs to say goodbye to him.

'I'll be back Friday night,' he said, giving me a quick kiss on the cheek, and with a wave of his hand he was gone, driving off down the lane, and I was alone.

Mrs Savino arrived later on that morning. She was a friendly woman, with a warm smile. 'Nice to meet you, Ellie. Zak says I'm to take good care of you,' she said, taking her basket of fresh milk and bread into the kitchen. She brewed coffee and, as we sat in the yard to drink it, she gave me a run-down of the location, not once asking me any questions about myself. With her in the house I felt happy and safe, but when she left I began to feel lonely and a little scared on my own.

That evening, as I gazed out of my bedroom window, I longed to walk along the shore and paddle in the blue, inviting sea. But I was scared that if I stepped outside the door a cop would grab me and cart me off to a detention centre.

When it grew dark, I stepped out on to the lawn and stood looking up at the stars and the moon, listening to the sound of the crickets, filled with a sense of loneliness and longing for Zak's return.

The following morning, I ventured down the little lane to the shore. I kept looking over my shoulder to make sure there was no one following me. At the water's edge I took off my shoes and, holding up my skirt, waded in. To my surprise the water was cold.

I continued along on the beach, walking out my frustration and anger at Uncle Jack for ruining everything, and wondering how I would continue with the constant threat of him in the background.

Mrs Savino was at the house when I returned. 'You're not eating much,' she said, looking into the fridge.

'I'm sorry, I'm not very hungry.'

Her eyes were kind as she looked at me. 'Let me fix

you some breakfast. You look as if you could do with a little nourishment.' She immediately began cracking eggs into a bowl. 'Shouldn't you be at school, or at work or somethin'?' she asked as she whisked them.

'I have to stay here for a while,' I said, turning away, humiliated at my predicament.

'Oh!' She shot me a curious glance, but asked no further questions.

When she'd gone I felt lonelier than ever. Nice as the place was, I longed for the clutter of my own little room, with my own things around me. I even missed my bits of material heaped up in the corner. Most of all I missed work. I'd have given anything to be back at Duchamp, making my hats.

The next day, Mrs Savino said, 'I'm going to the library this afternoon if you feel like coming with me. There's nothing like a good book to pass the time.'

'I'd love to come,' I said, jumping at the opportunity.

While at the library I spied a book on book-keeping. Thinking that it would be useful if I were ever to start my own business, I borrowed it, and bought a ledger in a nearby store. That afternoon I began to study it.

From then on, the time flew by and I didn't feel so lonely any more. In the evenings I took long walks, even going as far as the port itself to look at the storefronts. I noticed that the stores were smaller, more exclusive versions of the Boston ones. I thought of Violet and longed to see her and talk to her. I missed Shirlee too and wondered how Mr Samuel had taken her news.

Zak returned on Friday night, full of apologies for being late. 'Got delayed at meetings,' he said, hugging me. Later, noticing the ledger with my neat column of figures, he said with an amused smile, 'So you found something to keep the boredom at bay.'

'I thought I'd learn how to balance books, for when I have my own business,' I said. 'I'm planning on going to night school and doing a course in business studies as soon as I've finished my apprenticeship – if I ever get that far,' I said forlornly.

'I've been thinking . . .' Zak began.

'Yes?'

'Let's get married,' he finished casually.

'Married? Are you serious?'

'Never more so. If you and I were married, I'd be your next of kin. That way your Uncle Jack would have no rights over you whatsoever.'

I looked at him in amazement. 'You'd be willing to marry me just so I could get rid of Uncle Jack?'

'And also to prove to you once and for all that Gloria is not part of my plans for the future.'

Flabbergasted, I said, 'That's very sweet of you, Zak, but it isn't reason enough for us to get married.'

He took me in his arms. 'I care about you, Ellie. I can give you the security you need to start afresh.'

I stood back and, taking a deep breath said, 'I care about you, too, Zak, but I can't marry you. I'm too young, for one thing, and I really don't fit into your life.'

'What do you mean?'

'I'm not sophisticated enough.'

Zak hushed me with a kiss. 'Don't talk nonsense.'

'And I don't understand stocks and bonds.'

He laughed. 'You don't have to understand my business to marry me. Ellie! Stop putting up all these obstacles. I'm crazy about you. We're made for each other and that's all that matters.'

'But what will your parents have to say? I'm Roman Catholic, you're Jewish.'

'I don't need their permission,' he said crossly. 'And I'm willing to be married in your church. To prove it let's go see the local priest tomorrow, make the arrangements for a quiet wedding here in Hyannis.'

'But Zak, you can't do that without letting your parents know.'

'Why not?' He took me in his arms. 'I'll tell them when it's all arranged.'

'What if they disapprove of me?' I protested.

But he hushed me with a long, lingering kiss.

The following day was gloriously sunny as we walked through an alleyway to a blue, clapboard chapel overlooking the bay. The stillness of the sea and the green of the trees held a spellbinding beauty. Zak went to the presbytery door and rang the bell. A young priest in a cassock answered.

'Can I help you?' he asked with a pleasant smile.

'I'm Zak Rubens and this is Eleanor O'Rourke, we'd like to get married in your church,' he said.

Puzzled, he looked from one of us to the other. 'Are you Roman Catholics,' he asked.

'I am,' I said.

'I'm Jewish' Zak told him. 'But I'm quite willing to be married in the Catholic Church. We would like a quiet wedding, and as soon as possible.'

'Why the rush?'

'Because we're in love and we want to be together,' Zak said lamely.

The priest turned to me, 'You'll need the consent of a parent or guardian,' he said, a little suspiciously.

I looked at Zak in his handmade shirt and neat slacks, and it struck me how unsuited we looked standing there together, and how it would take some convincing to fool the priest about our motives for this marriage.

To Zak he said, 'You'll need a licence, and there's a waiting period while the banns are read out.'

Disappointed, Zak said that he would return as soon as possible with all the necessary papers.

'He didn't believe us. He thinks I'm pregnant,' I said as soon as the priest shut the door on us.

Zak looked drained as he mopped his brow. 'If only

he knew . . .' he said and, with an exasperated sigh, added, 'I suppose we'll have to tell my parents.'

'We've no choice in the matter,' I agreed.

The following Sunday Zak drove me to his home in Boston to introduce me to his parents. At first his father was charming, and his mother was elegant and welcoming. We were midway through a delicious lunch of lobster salad at the beautifully laid table when Zak turned to his parents and said with a smile, 'Dad, Mom, I've got something to tell you.'

Mrs Rubens looked up sharply from her plate. Mr Rubens continued eating.

'I've asked Ellie to marry me and she's agreed. We would like your blessing,' Zak said.

Mr Rubens slowly put down his knife and fork and focused his sharp, suspicious eyes on Zak. 'And how did you come to this decision?' he asked, a baffled expression on his face.

'We've fallen in love.'

'Oh! I see! And that makes it OK to rush out and get married.'

'It's what we want,' Zak said, turning to me with a smile.

'Marriage is too drastic a step, you two hardly know one another,' his father said impatiently.

Zak said quietly, 'We fully intend to go through with it, Dad.'

'Are you crazy? Don't you realise that a marriage of this kind would be totally unsuitable.' Throwing down his napkin, Mr Rubens got to his feet.

Zak stood up and faced him. 'We've been to see the priest at Hyannis.'

At that, Mr Rubens' face turned crimson. With eyes full of anger he said, 'In my office, now.' He stormed off, Zak following him.

I heard Mr Rubens' raised voice. 'You're a naïve fool letting your head be turned by a pretty girl who's out for her own gains. Is that the best you can do, throw yourself away on a romantic dream? Don't you realise that marriage is for life? You'll never be able to get out of it once you've made those vows.'

I recoiled into my chair while Mrs Rubens sat rigid, pretending that nothing out of the ordinary was happening.

Zak returned, his face red with rage. 'Come on, Ellie, let's get out of here,' he said, taking me by the hand.

We left, followed by a scowling Mr Rubens. 'You're making the biggest mistake of your life,' he called after us in an outraged voice.

'He won't stop us,' Zak vowed as we drove back to Hyannis Port. 'We'll get married in a Registry Office. I'm not waiting around for his approval.'

I tried to imagine us in that tiny chapel, both of us standing before an embarrassed priest, no family or friends to share our special day – and couldn't.

Zak left for work early the next morning still determined to marry me, regardless of his parents' opposition.

Twenty

L ate one afternoon, I looked out of the window to see a sleek black car coming down the road. It stopped outside the house. Terrified that Uncle Jack had found me again, I ran to the door, bolted it, then peeped out from behind the drapes of my bedroom window. A man and a woman got out: the man in a dark suit and a trilby hat with the brim tilted, the woman dazzling in a glamorous blue coat and turban to match. As they stopped to check the number on the post box I realised that it was Mr Samuel and Shirlee.

I ran downstairs and rushed to open the door. 'Shirlee!' I cried. 'Oh, I can't believe it's you,' I said, welcoming her with outstretched arms while Mr Samuel stood rigid at the door.

Starry-eyed, her cheeks glowing, she laughed delightedly. 'Ellie, it's so good to see ya. We're on our honeymoon. Thought we'd run down to see how you're gettin' on. Violet gave us the address. We took a gamble on finding ya in.'

'Why, congratulations!' I said, thrilled at seeing them

both again. 'I hope you'll both be very happy.'

'We will,' he said, looking at Shirlee as if he could never get enough of her.

'We was worried about ya, weren't we Sam?' Shirlee's glance rested on him a second.

'We sure were,' he said.

'That was a terrible thing that horrible ol' uncle of yours went and did. If I'd only known I'd have stopped him, and no mistake,' Mr Samuel said, relaxing into an armchair. I hardly recognised him for the man who'd kept us all at arm's length in the factory. There wasn't a sign of that authority in him now. He was like an old friend.

'I hated having to leave town,' I said. 'And I was so sorry to have let Mr Duchamp down.'

Mr Samuel said consolingly, 'I've had a word with him. He understands that it's not your fault. He says his clients are coming in asking for you every day. Wants to know if you're planning on returning to Boston. There's big demand for your hats by all accounts . . .' He paused. 'Miss O'Rourke – Ellie – I've got a proposition for you.'

'You have?'

'Would you consider working for me? I could supply you with premises and all the equipment you would need to make your very own hats.'

I thought I was hearing things. 'Why would you do this for me?' I asked, surprised.

'I'm a businessman, Ellie, and with my contacts I

could introduce your hats into the best fashion stores in Boston. This is the prime selling time for fashion houses in Boston. There are extremely wealthy people who will pay through the nose for something really special at the start of the season. Your hats will bring that element of perfection to the opera, the ballet, and concerts. Not only for night-time wear, but daytime too.'

'I can't go back to Boston. Uncle Jack would find me there . . .' I gulped back my tears.

Mr Samuel clenched his fists. 'Of course you can. You leave that bully to me. If he comes looking for you again, I'll take care of him.' Mr Samuel's eyes caught mine and held them. In that second I realised he meant every word. Somehow he knew a way of dealing with Uncle Jack and he wasn't going to say what it was.

'This would be a great opportunity for me, Mr Samuel, and I'm very grateful,' I said, 'but how about you rent me the space so that the business is mine.' Thinking fast I added, 'In return, I'd give you a share of the profit that I'd make.'

Mr Samuel looked a little taken aback at this request. But just when I thought that I'd blown my chances with him he turned his clear eyes on me and said, 'I'll make a deal with you. I'll rent you the space, supply the material, and buy the hats from you wholesale. That'll give us both what we want, you a business, me a good profit margin. What'd you say?'

'That would be perfect, Mr Samuel.'

He smiled. 'As long as you realise the responsibility that you're taking on. You'll have to put in all the hard work.'

'I'm not afraid of hard work.'

'Good,' said Mr Samuel. As we all shook hands I had to hold myself back from jumping for joy.

I went to make the coffee. Shirlee followed me into the kitchen. 'Isn't he just darlin',' she said.

'He sure is,' I agreed, still reeling from the shock of our conversation.

Lowering her voice, she said, 'When I told him my news it didn't bother him in the least. He said that he needed someone to calm him down, and that I need somebody strong like him to decide things. We're just right for each other, Ellie!'

'I'm so glad for you, Shirlee. You deserve the best.'

'Thank you. I can't believe my luck.'

'Where will you be living?'

'At Sam's bachelor pad for now. We'll buy our own place and start over when the baby comes. Oh, I'm so happy, Ellie.'

'And I'm happy for you,' I said.

After a quick cup of coffee, Mr Samuel patted his fob watch and said, 'Come on, Shirl, we'd better get going, we've got some sightseeing to do.' On their way out he said to me, 'I'll come to take you back to Boston as soon as I've found you a new apartment.'

Full of pride in his new bride, he led her down the

steps. I waved until their car faded far away into the misty evening, and then I sat down and gave myself up to delicious thoughts about my having my very own hat business in Boston. The idea of it didn't scare me. With an opportunity like the one I'd just been given, there was nothing to stop me. I couldn't wait to tell Zak so I phoned him at work.

'Guess what happened today, Zak,' I burst out. Not waiting for his reply, I carried on. 'Mr Samuel and Shirlee came to see me. Mr Samuel is going to rent me a store he owns in Boston. He says he'll deal with Uncle Jack if he tries to kidnap me again. It'll be ready for the start of the season. 'What'd you think?' I blabbed on, unable to contain my excitement.

'Ellie, your voice is muffled, I can't hear you properly.'

'Sorry, perhaps it's the reception out here . . . You don't sound very enthusiastic.'

'I've got a lot of things on my mind right now.'

'Like what?' I asked.

'Business stuff. I'll tell you when I see you.'

'OK—' But the line went dead – we must have been cut off. I expected Zak to call me right back, but he didn't. I frowned, wondering what I might have said to upset him . . .

'So, what's on your mind?' I asked Zak anxiously, soon after he walked through the door the following Saturday.

'Well, it so happens I'm being transferred to head office in Washington. It's quite a promotion. A great opportunity.'

'That's wonderful news, Zak, congratulations.' I threw my arms around him.

'Thanks Ellie,' he said beaming. 'I knew you'd be pleased. Now we can get married without the interference of my parents.'

'But I can't go to Washington . . . What about Mr Samuel's offer?' I said breathlessly.

'Cancel it. You don't need to work. I'll be making a good living for both of us.'

I laughed, thinking that he was joking.

'I'm serious. Ellie, the wives of stockbrokers don't work,' he said firmly.

'But, Zak, it's all arranged. Mr Samuel is fixing it all up for me.'

'Well, I'm sure he'll understand when you tell him that we're getting married and moving to Washington.'

'So you want me to throw away everything I've worked for just to get married?' I said furiously.

'You're a woman, and a woman can't have a business and a husband and do right by both. Besides, I can't have my colleagues thinking that I'm not able to support a wife!'

'I'm proud of my work, it's real important to me, Zak.'

'Of course you are, but you could hardly consider it

as important as becoming my wife. I can give you far more than you'll ever earn in the hat trade.'

'But it's not about the money . . . I won't quit work to become your wife, Zak. I have hopes and dreams of my own. I can't throw them away,' I said, indignantly.

There was a silence, then Zak said, 'I take it you've decided not to marry me, then.'

'Not if it means having to give up my dream,' I said resolutely.

'Well, I hope you won't regret your decision. What if it doesn't work out for you?' he said, with a superior smile.

Hurt, I said, 'Thanks for your vote of confidence.'

We finished our meal arguing, and continued arguing for the rest of the weekend, getting nowhere. By the time Zak left on the Monday morning we were barely civil to one another.

'Perhaps we should both take a break from each other for a while?' I said sadly.

Reluctantly, he agreed that it might be for the best and left quickly.

When Shirlee phoned me a few days later to let me know that she and Mr Samuel were back from their honeymoon, I told her about Zak's promotion and that I'd turned down his marriage proposal.

'You did! I think you're crazy. Can't you see how rich he's gonna be?' she said.

'But what about my hats?'

'You can always do a little trade from home when you're settled,' she suggested.

'That wouldn't be enough for me. I'd be bored within a week, Shirlee.'

'Well, you can't stay on in Hyannis now. Get the afternoon train back to Boston tomorrow. I'll come pick you up.'

'I can't impose myself on you, Shirlee.'

'I'll get Sam to fix up your place pronto,' she said.

Before I left Hyannis Port, I phoned Zak to tell him that I was returning to Boston and to thank him for all his kindness to me. In a voice that was cool and distant he wished me well in my new venture. On the day I was leaving, Mrs Savino came to the station with me to see me off. 'Write and let me know how you're doin',' she said as she hugged me goodbye. I promised her that I would.

True to her word, Shirlee met me at the station and took me straight to a miserable-looking narrow house, near the factory. The door was padlocked. As I pressed my head against the glass, trying to get a glimpse of the interior, Mr Samuel arrived.

'It won't take long to renovate,' he said, as I gazed at the dingy walls. 'You can decorate it whatever way you want it,' he said, letting us in.

The place was surprisingly nice inside, though.

Downstairs there was a long, airy room with a large table, a heater and two chairs. Upstairs there was a tiny kitchen and a bedroom. All my belongings were already installed.

'It's perfect,' I exclaimed, clearing my throat so I wouldn't disgrace myself and cry.

'Well, it's a start,' Mr Samuel said.

'It's more than that, it's wonderful. I know I can make something of this place,' I said resolutely.

Shirlee grabbed hold of me and, as we did a little dance around the floor, I felt like a child in my very own sweet shop.

Mr Samuel laughed. Regaining his composure he said, 'This is the right time to be in business, Ellie. There's a lot of money about, and plenty of people who want to spend it.' Later, over lunch, he said, 'To start with, I want you to make a practical-style hat for the winter. The days are growing cold.'

I took out my sketchpad and sketched a close-fitting felt hat with a tilt over the eyebrow, explaining to him that the band and trimmings would be the choice of the customer.

'How much will it retail at?' he asked.

'Twelve dollars,' I said, going on the prices Mr Duchamp charged for a similar hat.

'Good profit there,' he said.

I knew he was right but that night, when I was alone in my new surroundings, I started thinking about what

I'd taken on and fear replaced the excitement I'd felt earlier on.

The next morning I went to the millinery supply shop to purchase all the necessities to make a start. I began by making a sample hat, a standard-size deep felt cloche which I thought would be easy for Mr Samuel to sell, and stayed up late that night finishing it so that I could show it to him the next day.

'It's just what we want,' he said, when he saw it. He loved the way it flattered the face and hugged the head for warmth. 'Make a dozen of them as fast as you can,' he said.

As soon as the hats were sold, Mr Samuel paid me my share of the profit and gave me a further order. I put the money in a cash box towards the rent and materials and food, and set to work again, only faster this time.

After I'd paid Mr Samuel the rent each week, I barely had enough money left over for food and heat. Sometimes, Shirlee would bring in some delicious leftovers from dinner the previous night, but mostly I survived on eggs and beans.

I made sample hats for window displays in various outlets. Orders came flooding in so fast that I had to rush out and buy more stock and materials from the supply store. The hats sold quickly. Even the sample hats sold to women who insisted that they couldn't wait for the next batch.

Often I worked until the early hours, finishing the orders for the following day. Shirlee came in some mornings to do the machining while I concentrated on the fine stitching and decorations. When she'd leave, I would work on alone into the night. Before going to bed I'd tick off the orders, write the amount of money I was owed into my ledger, then drag myself upstairs to bed.

I worked harder than ever and tried not to think about Zak. Violet came to see me. 'I've missed you so much, Ellie,' she said.

'I missed you too. I'm so glad to be back in Boston,' I said, proudly showing her around.

'It's wonderful,' she said. 'Let's go dancing to celebrate. It'll be like old times.'

'Sounds lovely, but I haven't got the energy,' I confessed.

Instead we sat in my little kitchen sipping coffee. I told her about another of my hectic days and she told me all her news.

'How's Zak?' I asked cautiously.

'He seems to be lonely. I think he misses you, Ellie.' She looked at me.

'I miss him too,' I admitted to her.

'Perhaps you should call him, or send him a note.'

'What's the point? We'll only end up arguing again.'

'Well, if you keep working this hard without a break you won't survive,' she warned.

'I want to prove to Zak that I'm serious about my trade. Besides, the excitement of my business will keep me going.'

The orders came faster than I could cope with. I worked later and later each evening. Shirlee, by now heavily pregnant and tired, wanted to spend more time at home with her feet up, so I decided to employ an apprentice. Shirlee suggested that I ask Dora.

I knew Dora had a gift for decorating hats. I'd seen her jazz up a plain turban to make it look a million dollars. She was delighted with the offer, and glad to leave the factory. When I decided to incorporate a turban of my own style into my range, Dora and I decorated the finished product with imitation fruit and beads. This was time consuming, but it was worth it to see the finished product. Those hats became favourites among the younger customers, so Mr Samuel told me.

As the business grew Mr Samuel received requests for hats for special occasions such as weddings, engagements and christenings. Dora and I were kept busy all of the time.

We'd been in business a couple of months when the telephone rang one morning.

'Hello Ellie, it's Zak,' the voice said.

'Zak!' I said, shocked at hearing from him after all this time.

'I'm back in town. I'd like to see you, Ellie. May I call for you tonight, at eight?'

I tried to keep my voice casual as I said, 'That would be lovely,' and immediately spun into a panic of what to say, what to wear.

He arrived at the store with a dozen red roses. 'Peace offering,' he said, shyly.

'Thank you, Zak, they're beautiful.' I wanted to throw my arms around him, and hug him, but I held myself back. Instead I followed his eyes around my workroom as he surveyed it.

'It's nice,' was all he said, but I could see that he was impressed. Turning back to me he said, 'But you look as if you haven't eaten a square meal in ages.'

'It's all the hard work,' I laughed.

'Give yourself a night off tonight. I'm taking you out to dinner.'

'But I've so much to do . . .'

He raised his hand. 'No excuses. Besides, there is a new restaurant at the harbour that I want to try out.'

Over dinner, Zak told me excitedly about his position in Washington, and his increasing stocks and debentures there. Then he turned to me and asked with a smile, 'So, have you had your fill of the struggle of trying to make ends meet yet, Ellie?'

'It's not such a struggle now. I'm doing very well,' I said defensively.

'But it's so tough, your business, and you'll never be able to compete with the big stores,' he said.

'I'm not trying to. I'm creating my own niche in the market, and establishing my name as a milliner,' I explained.

There was a pause while he studied me. 'Does that mean you won't be coming to Washington with me?' he asked.

'I'm not going to give up my business, Zak,' I said firmly.

'And I won't give up asking you to marry me,' he said, just as firmly.

I blushed. 'Please let's not argue. It's all we ever seem to do when we're together, and I hate it.'

'Fine,' he said and the rest of the meal was spent in virtual silence. Zak dropped me off at my door at the end of the evening, promising to keep in touch, but he drove off with an air of injured pride.

With a heavy heart I started work the next morning, Zak's face before me all of the time. Everything went wrong. The flowers and feather went on the wrong hats; the orders got mixed up. I was angry with him for his unreasonable demands and angrier with myself for letting it interfere with my work.

★ ★ ★

Shirlee gave birth to a bouncing baby boy. She named him David, after Mr Samuel's father, and spent all her time taking care of him. When I went to visit her in her new mansion on Beacon Hill she greeted me joyfully, David in her arms. 'Isn't he a beaut?' she said, her eyes shining with pride, her face soft with love as she cradled him.

Shirlee guarded her baby like a lioness, and spoke to his nanny in definite tones. I noticed that since she'd become Mrs Samuel she was more confident and quick to pass judgement on everything. 'Sam says that the store's getting too cramped for your requirements.'

'It is, but it'll have to do for now. I can't afford the downtown prices.'

'I'll get him to keep an eye out for a bargain for you,' she promised.

The harder I worked, the less often I thought of Zak. Occasionally, when I did think about him, I'd wonder if the haughty Gloria was still lurking in the background waiting for him, and a vague sense of panic would rise up in me.

As the business expanded, I needed more space. Also, I wanted to rent a store of my own with a workroom attached. I started saving for a rental deposit on a store, and was looking to find the right one when Mr Samuel came to tell me that Uncle Jack had been back in Boston searching for me.

'His trail of enquiries led him to me, but don't worry,

I sent him off with a severe warning not to return,' he said, seeing the consternation in my face.

'Thank you, Mr Samuel,' I said gratefully.

He smiled. 'It was a pleasure,' he said. 'He asked me to give you this.' He handed me a letter from Johnny. Then, with a look of concern, he said, 'By the way your Uncle Jack mentioned that your mother hadn't been well, and that's why he wanted to contact you.'

A stab of fear shot through me. 'Did he say what was wrong with her?'

'No, he didn't. It might have been his excuse to come here.'

As soon as he left, I tore open the envelope.

Dear Ellie

I haven't heard from you in a long time, and I don't understand why. I keep thinking of all sorts of reasons as to why you haven't written, and can't come up with any answers. If you're in trouble let me know and I'll help you. I went to see your mother yesterday. She is very concerned about you as she doesn't have any idea of your whereabouts or how to go about looking for you.

If you receive this letter, please write back and just tell us how you are. I would give anything to see you walking across the fields this very minute.

Meantime, I remain,

Your faithful friend,

Johnny

As I read it, I longed for the sight of home: the open fields, and the perfect tranquillity. A tear dropped on the page as a feeling of homesickness swept over me. I longed to see Mam, Lucy and Ed. I longed to meet my baby brother, and catch up with Johnny Sheerin, and Brendan, and all of the neighbours. I thought of Boston, and the hot summer ahead here.

'What I wouldn't give to spend a cool summer day in Ireland,' I said to Mr Samuel.

'I hear it's a very beautiful country,' he said.

'Yes it is, especially where I come from.' I turned to him. 'I've got to go home, Mr Samuel.'

'But what about the business?' he asked, anxiously.

'I'll leave you in charge of it,' I said boldly. 'Dora and I will work hard to finish the outstanding orders and you can hold further orders until I get back. Tell the clients that I've taken a holiday and that I'll be back soon.'

'You're due a holiday,' he agreed.

I booked my passage home, and spent the rest of the month fulfilling as many orders as possible.

Twenty-One

I was back in Ireland at last. Cobh looked exactly the same with the little houses curving up the hill, the queues of immigrants waiting to embark on the *Mauritania*, the ship I'd travelled home on.

At the port I hired a sidecar and driver to take me back to Lisheen. Every passing detail on the journey enthralled me; the white hawthorn on the hedgerows, fleeting birds across the fields. Rounding the corner of Lisheen, I caught my first glimpse of the sparkling sea and the fishing boats. The village was quiet. There was no one about. As we approached our farm the scent of the fields wafted towards me. A curl of smoke rose up from the cottage. I was home.

At the gate I paid the driver, took my suitcase, and walked up the path between the flower borders. The cottage looked spick and span with a fresh coat of whitewash. Early roses trailed round the door. As I passed the laurel bush, Shep came rushing towards me barking madly.

'Shep!' I knelt down to pet him. Shivering with

excitement, he followed me into the yard where the hens were pecking. Neat rows of vegetables led all the way to the orchard. As I stood inhaling the familiar scent of turf smoke, Mam's voice called out, 'That you Ed?'

Nervously, I approached the back door. Mam was sitting by the range. 'Hello Mam,' I said softly.

She turned. 'Ellie!' Her hands flew to her mouth. She got to her feet. 'Is it you? Is it really you!' she cried.

'Yes, Mam, it's me,' I said, rooted to the spot.

'Glory be to God!' Not another word passed between us as she stood gazing at me, taking me in, so that there was no question or doubt that I was truly standing before her. She'd aged. Her hair was greyer, and her skin was taut across her cheekbones.

I went to her and she enveloped me in her arms. We stood holding each other and crying. Eventually we drew apart. 'I can't believe it. I'd given up hope of ever seeing you again. And here you are.' She gazed at me as she said, 'It was terrible not hearing from you for so long, knowing nothing about you. I thought you were dead. A rush of tears ran down her face. In that split second I saw the depth of her grief. I wanted to run from the cottage and hide with the terrible guilt I felt for what I'd put her through.

Wiping her eyes, she said, 'You must be famished after your journey,' and went to put the kettle on and get out the battered cake tin.

'Where's Matthew?'

'He's sleeping. And Lucy's over at Mabel's.'

When the tea came, I had to use both hands to steady my cup as I drank it.

'You're certainly a beautiful girl now, Ellie, but very thin. You haven't been looking after yourself properly? Have you been eating enough?'

'I'm well, Mam. I've been working hard, that's all.'

She nodded, her searching eyes on me.

'I'm sorry for causing you so much anguish.' I bowed my head in shame.

'Why did you do it, Ellie? Why did you run away?' she asked.

'I'd no opportunity where I was.' I told her about the cruelty I'd suffered at the hands of Uncle Jack and Aunt Sally.

'But Alice fared all right,' she said, perplexed.

'When Alice went to school I stayed in the home, doing all the work, Mam. I wanted more, for myself.'

'You should have written to us and let us know you were unhappy, instead of running away like that, Ellie. We could have done something about it.' Her face crumpled so sadly that I could hardly bear to look at her. 'I blame myself, I should never have let you go off like that, to think of you all by yourself in Boston . . .' She raised her arms towards me as if asking me for forgiveness.

'It wasn't your fault Mam, and I wasn't on my own.'

I told her all about making friends with Violet and Zak on the ship, and how Violet had invited me stay with her family. 'I managed fine, Mam. I got a job in a shirt factory. A girl named Shirlee took me under her wing. I did well, I was lucky to get out. Most of the girls in that factory will spend the rest of their lives slaving away for a pittance.' I was telling her about the wonderful opportunity that Mr Samuel had given me when I heard a baby's cry.

'Matthew!'

'He doesn't like being left alone for long,' she said, hurrying into the bedroom, me following her.

In the old cot, under the window, a beautiful little boy stood clutching the bars. 'This is your baby brother. Isn't he the image of your father?' There was intense pride in her voice and adoration in her eyes as she picked him up. 'This is your big sister, Ellie, darlin'.' He looked at me with inquisitive eyes like Dad's.

'Hello Matthew.' My fingers trembled as I touched his cheek.

'Here, you take him,' she said, lifting him out and handing him to me.

I carried him back to the kitchen and sat him on my knee. His presence shifted the awkward atmosphere that had been there. The ache that had been in my heart since Dad's death seemed to ease as I held him, while Mam filled the milk pan and set it on the range. He smiled and dribbled at me.

There was the sound of wheels coming into the yard, voices and laughter.

'That'll be Ed now, and his girl, Maura Connolly. She's one of the Connollys from Monk's Cross. She's a nice girl and has the makings of a good housekeeper,' Mam said. 'There's someone here to see you, Ed,' she called, going to the door.

Ed came in, followed by a pretty, dark-haired girl.

'Hello Ed,' I said, tearfully.

He looked at me, hardly believing his eyes. 'Ellie! Where did you spring from?'

'She's just arrived,' Mam said, taking Matthew from me to feed him.

Ed gave me a bear hug. 'Great to see you. You had us all worried.'

'I'm sorry.'

'You must have fared out well. Not many come back from America,' he said, eyeing my elegant clothes.

'Yes, and I thought I'd take a holiday,' I said lightly.

He introduced me to Maura, who said, 'You'll be here for our wedding, I hope.'

'Wedding!' I looked from one to the other excitedly. 'When?'

'It's in three weeks' time,' Ed said.

Maura looked at him. 'We could move the date forward, I suppose. It's not as if it's going to be a grand affair. It's just family.'

'Thanks, Maura,' Ed said, giving her a kiss on the cheek.

Watching them standing there, full of happiness as they talked about their plans for their small wedding, lifted my spirits even more.

After they left I walked through the rooms, touching the walls, running my hand along the furniture. In our bedroom I looked at Alice's empty bed and let the tears run down my cheeks at the thought of her, all by herself, so far away from home.

Later, when Matthew was tucked up in bed and Mam was quietly knitting, I let myself out off through the back door and walked across the fields to Johnny Sheerin's farm.

It was a beautiful evening, with a soft purple mist on the hills and a slanting light over the fields. There was no one in at Sheerin's cottage so I continued on down to the shore to look for him.

The fishing boats were lined up against the jetty. Brendan Sheerin, with his horse, was carting sand, slowly, as if he had all the time in the world. When he caught sight of me he said, startled, 'Ellie O'Rourke!'

'Hello Brendan. Where's Johnny?'

'He's over by the rocks mending his boat,' he said.

I heard the sound of a hammering as I approached. Johnny, in his green waders, was fixing a plank of wood on to the side of his upturned fishing boat. I couldn't believe how my heart was racing at seeing him again.

'Hello Johnny.'

'Ellie!' He stopped what he was doing and stood gazing at me as if I was an apparition.

There was an awkward pause as we stood at the water's edge, surrounded by lobster pots and netting, the tide lapping gently around us.

'You came back.'

And beneath his matter-of-fact greeting I detected his nerves.

He put down his hammer and approached me in that hesitant way of his, and shook my hand, his eyes on me as if he expected me to disappear at any minute.

'I was afraid that I might never see you again.' The relief in his voice left me in no doubt that he'd longed for this reunion.

'Well, here I am,' I said brightly, tears stinging my eyes.

'You've cut your hair.'

'Yes.'

'Suits you.'

A far-off gull gave an eerie cry. A cold wind blew up suddenly. 'Come on up to the cottage,' he said.

The cottage was newly decorated. The old black range in the kitchen was gone and a new cream-coloured Aga stood in its place. There was a big white sink with a chromium tap, and a new wooden table and chairs in the centre. 'You like it?' he asked.

'It's beautiful, Johnny.'

'I did it all myself. It took a while.'

He filled the kettle, put out a neat little cup and saucer with flowers on it for me, and a blue delft mug for himself. It was awkward sitting down, trying to make conversation.

'You stopped writing.' Though there was no reprimand in his voice I knew he felt hurt.

'I meant to write to you as soon as I got to Boston but I was scared that Uncle Jack would find out where I was.' He nodded. 'As it turned out, he did find me,' I added.

I told Johnny everything. I even told him about Zak and how he'd been willing to marry me to give me legal status in the States. Johnny showed no surprise. 'Why didn't you marry him, and live happily ever after?' he asked, as though he didn't care.

'Everything went against us, and, to be truthful, I guess I wasn't ready to settle down and spend the rest of my life entertaining Washington's high society. I had dreams of my own for the future.'

Johnny smiled. 'You always had dreams, Ellie.'

I smiled back at him. 'I'd better go home or Mam'll think I've disappeared again.'

'That would never do,' he said, getting to his feet.

Johnny walked me home through the fields as he'd always done, but he wasn't at ease as before. He was distant, even shy of me.

In the yard he said, 'Would you like to come fishing with me tomorrow?'

I hesitated. 'I haven't been out in a boat since . . .' I stopped, looking doubtfully at him.

'You don't have to come, but I'd like you to.'

'And I'd like to,' I said, and went home to Mam, who was waiting up for me.

Twenty-Two

There was a mist around the sea the following day, a sign of the heat to come. Johnny was waiting for me in the boat. 'Hop in,' he said, reaching out his hand. I gripped it and stepped in. Johnny pushed off with one of the oars.

The oars made a rhythmic sound as we rowed out into the wider water. As we approached Rocky Island I saw the wild flowers growing in the crevices of the rocks, close to where Dad had drowned, and turned away sadly.

As soon as we landed at the tiny dock, Johnny unloaded his fishing gear while I spread out the rug.

The heat rose and Johnny said, 'Let's go for a swim.' He dived in and swam off with powerful strokes. I circled the rocks for a little while then got out and lay on my towel, letting the sun dry me as I took in every detail of the landscape and the sky, savouring the fact that nothing had changed. I watched Johnny swimming in the distance, and wished that he'd turn and come back. How unbearable it would be if he too were to drown.

Eventually, he returned and stretched out on the rug beside me. 'I was getting anxious about you, swimming out so far,' I said.

He laughed. 'No fear of me. Sure, didn't I give you your first swimming lesson, remember?'

'I'll never forget, you nearly let me drown.'

'I did not.' The years seemed to drop away and we were like children again, bickering like we'd always done.

While he fished I sunbathed, listening to the familiar sounds of the gulls and the waves slapping against the rocks. Gradually, I began to relax.

Johnny returned noisily with his catch of perch, gutted and cleaned, ready to cook. 'Time to eat, sleepyhead,' he said, tousling my hair and waking me up.

Expertly he built a fire, and he placed a large stone on either side of it, and a grill on the top. Soon, the delicious smell of roasting fish wafted through the air tantalisingly.

'Let's eat,' said Johnny. He removed one of the fish from the fire, placed one between slices of buttered soda bread, and handed it to me.

As we ate our delicious meal, we talked about Ed and Maura and their forthcoming wedding. 'Ed's a new man since he met Maura,' Johnny said, 'and he's done wonders with the farm.'

'So I've noticed.'

'Your Mam seems much better these days, too,' Johnny said.

'Was she very ill?'

'Well, she had a sort of nervous breakdown when she discovered . . .' He stopped, and looked at me.

'When she discovered what, Johnny?'

He hesitated. 'Discovered the circumstances of your dad's death.'

I looked at him sharply. 'What do you mean?'

'Didn't she tell you?'

'Tell me what?'

He looked away. It was difficult to know what he was thinking because I couldn't see his face.

'Johnny, tell me. I want to know.'

He turned to me. 'There's no easy way of saying this, Ellie. Your da's death wasn't an accident.'

'Are you saying that someone *killed* him?'

His eyes met mine. 'Yes,' he said.

'But why would anyone do that? Dad wasn't involved in the fighting.'

'That was just it. His refusal to get involved made him the object of a lot of criticism. He was seen as the enemy in certain quarters. A rumour was spread that your dad was a police informer.'

'*What?*' I clamped my hand over my mouth, sick from the effect of this revelation.

'It was a punishment on your dad for not taking sides. They made up this story that he did it to get Ed off the hook.'

'But it doesn't make sense. Ed was sent to jail with the

others and, anyway, Dad wouldn't have done a thing like that.'

'They found out when it was too late.'

I buried my face in my hands and cried as I recalled the terrible night Dad had drowned and the screams of Mam when the knock came to the door. At that time the whole place had seethed with the secrets of furtive people in the community, even brother had fought against brother, neighbour against neighbour.

'Ellie, I'm so sorry. I shouldn't have told you.'

'No, I'm glad you did,' I sniffed, wiping my eyes. Johnny put his arms around me and tried to soothe me, but no words could smooth over this bitter truth. A shadow had been cast over our day out.

We washed our plates in the sea and packed up our things. Johnny rowed back in silence, slid the boat into its moorings. 'Take your bag, I'll manage the rest,' he said. I climbed out. The harbour was busy with fishermen unloading their cargo.

As we walked home, dusk was descending. At the yard we said good night to one another, subdued. The magical day we'd just shared was over and we were back in reality.

I didn't mention Johnny's revelation to Mam, but as I watched her rocking Matthew to sleep, singing him the lullaby that Dad used to sing to us, I mourned his loss all over again. I thought of how he'd press his face into her hair and sing, '*You are my heart's delight,*' and laugh when she'd push him, saying, 'Go on with you' teasingly.

Next day, I cycled over to Aunt Mabel's. Lucy came running to meet me. 'Ellie! Ellie!' she cried, falling into my arms.

Shocked by her height and her beauty, I couldn't take my eyes off of her. 'You're so grown up, Lucy,' I said, and she laughed, delightedly.

Aunt Mabel came out. Her delight at seeing me brightened up her gaunt face. 'Ed told us you were home. Just in time to help us with the wedding dress,' she said, leading the way into her workroom to show me the white satin sheath. An excited Lucy showed off the pink organdie bridesmaid's frock she was making for herself.

Over coffee I told them all about my adventures in America. Aunt Mabel smiled proudly as I talked about the hats I had been making for Boston's elite. Afterwards, while Mabel fitted the sleeves to the dress and Lucy did the hemming of her frock, I made a white lace headdress to hold the scalloped veil, and crowned it with pearl beading.

That night, when Lucy was in bed, I asked Aunt Mabel what she knew about the mystery of Dad's death. 'Is it true that he was killed?'

She looked shocked for a moment, then said, 'Who told you?'

'Johnny Sheerin. He thought I'd heard it from Mam.'

She looked away. 'It was a terrible thing that happened.'

'Tell me about it, Aunt Mabel. I don't want to ask Mam.'

'It's too awful to think about now,' she said.

'I have a right to know what you know about it, Aunt Mabel,' I insisted.

She straightened up, took a deep breath. 'Well, as you know, everyone assumed that it was an accident until eventually someone in the parish who knew the man responsible for your dad's death went to the police.'

I felt a cold shiver rising up from the pit of my stomach. 'Who did it?'

She tightened her lips. 'You wouldn't have known him, and it doesn't matter now anyway because he lost his own life in an ambush soon after that.' She sighed. 'Who could have seen it coming? Who would have thought that this could happen to a peace-loving man who was guilty of nothing more than minding his own business? A man who kept out of it all because he had a family and a farm to protect.'

'Johnny said Mam took it very badly.'

Aunt Mabel nodded. 'Her nerves got the better of her and she took to her bed. I thought she'd go crazy but, thankfully, she came round when Matthew was born.' With a strange look in her eyes she said, 'One thing it taught me is that you can trust no one.'

She looked at me with a critical eye. 'I thought your Mam would go under again when you disappeared.'

'I know, and I'm sorry,' I said guiltily.

Brightening up she said, 'With this moving around you've done, have you got the travelling bug out of your system yet?'

'No, not yet, why?'

'I was hoping that you'd stay here in Garrystown with me for a while.' Casting a sidelong glance at me she said, 'I could do with someone reliable like you to work with me. I get tired these days.' Her hand reached out to me. 'I'll be retiring one day, Ellie, and it'll all be yours.' Speechless, I looked at her. 'You're the daughter I never had.' She said it almost in a whisper, as if not having a daughter of her own was the most tragic thing that could have happened to her.

'Oh! Aunt Mabel, I don't know what to say.'

'Say yes. It's a thriving business, as you know,' she said, looking around.

I'd always placed great importance on Aunt Mabel's opinion. There was no one on earth would ever influence me as much as she'd done, and her desire to remodel me in her own image had worked. My eyes fell on the neat stack of folders with lists of customers, all sorted out in alphabetical order, and the neat rows of hats. I noticed how outdated they were compared to mine.

'I have to go back, Aunt Mabel.' I said, after a pause.

I felt bad at having to let her down when, obviously, she needed me, but I wasn't ready to stay, I hadn't got the adventure of America out of my system. Perhaps I never would.

'I'm sorry, Aunt Mabel. I've got to go back,' I repeated, trying to hold my tears back.

'I understand,' she said. 'You're young. You can't be expected to settle down here yet.'

I told her of my dreams to travel the world, to see London, Paris and Rome. She listened eagerly. 'You're right to go travelling. Here, you can get so far and no further, and, of course, we have the lovely begrudgers,' she said, patting my hand.

Twenty-Three

Maura walked slowly down the aisle on her father's arm to murmurs of 'beautiful' and 'gorgeous', to take her place beside Ed, her proud groom. Lucy trailed rose petals from a basket behind them. Smiling, they took their vows, looking as if they were made for one another. Mam wore a blue georgette suit that Aunt Mabel had made for her, and sat in the front pew with a white-satin-suited Matthew on her lap.

After the ceremony, we stepped out into the bright sunshine and stood in a group to be photographed, our frocks fluttering in the breeze. There was a joyous cheer and calls of 'Hey! You did it Ed,' and we all laughed happily, our earlier nerves gone. Johnny Sheerin, catching my eye, winked at me.

As soon as the photographs were taken, Aunt Mabel, stunning in a red raw-silk suit and matching brimmed cloche, pulled Ed close to her and said, 'I'm so proud of you.'

'Now smile for the camera,' Brendan Sheerin said, and everyone smiled at the Box Brownie.

Back at the cottage, Ed welcomed everyone and said, 'Did I hear anybody say they were thirsty?' A cheer went up.

'You'll have a glass of whiskey, won't you, Father?' Aunt Mabel asked Father Barry, the parish priest.

'Only a drop to toast the happy couple,' he said. He raised his glass as soon as she handed it to him. 'To Ed and Maura. May they have a long and happy life together,' he said.

We all cheered.

'I know we'll be happy.' Ed's eyes went lovingly to his rapturous bride. 'Now that the troubles are over, it's safe to live around here once more.' Everyone cheered. Ed continued, 'I would like us all to remember my Dad at this time. I know he'd approve of Maura, and the way things turned out.' Looking at me he said, 'And sure haven't we little to complain about now that Ellie is here, safe and sound.'

'Here, here,' Johnny said, raising his glass again.

Over the wedding breakfast, the talking went on in the usual, casual way about the economy and the burden on farmers to eke out a living. Aunt Mabel held forth on the shopping delights of her recent trip to London. She described the brocades and silks she had bought for her new collection.

Maura and Ed cut the wedding cake. Johnny, the best man, called for another toast to the bride and groom.

After the meal the tables were moved to one side. The Flynn brothers took out their violins. 'Let the dancing commence,' Peter Flynn said, as they tuned up. Maura and Ed started it off by waltzing around in a circle, everyone clapping them. Big farmers joined in and danced nimbly with their broad-hipped wives. Then Johnny swept me on to the floor, 'Like old times at the crossroads,' he said to the tune of 'The Irish Washerwoman'.

'I missed those dances more than anything,' I told him.

'I missed you,' Johnny said into my ear.

After we danced to my favourite tune, 'I'm Always Chasing Rainbows,' Johnny excused himself to everyone, saying that he was going to check the lobster pots.

'Must you go so soon?' I asked him.

'Come with me? Then I could walk you home.'

'I can't leave before the bride and groom,' I said, eyeing the stack of glasses mounting up at the sink.

'I'll be down at the shore. I'll wait for you,' he said and left.

'Shame he had to go,' Mam said looking after him.

'He has to check the lobster pots.'

'He could have got someone to do it for him,' Lucy said.

'He acted like he couldn't wait to get away,' Aunt Mabel cast a meaningful eye at me. 'Is there something going on between you two?'

'No, nothing at all.'

'We'll see.' She smiled secretively.

By the time Ed and Maura drove off in a sidecar they'd hired for a two-day honeymoon in Lisdoonvarna, the excitement of the day was over. When singing of the morbid, patriotic songs got underway I changed into a clean frock, brushed my hair, and took off to the shore. I found Johnny waiting by the boats.

'Come on, get in,' he said, untying the rope of the boat. As we rowed out silently in a path of moonlight, the oars made semicircle shapes on the water, smooth as silk. Every so often, a far-off gull cried out and another one answered. While Johnny checked each one of his pots and collected the lobsters into a cage, I trailed my hand in the water and looked up at the sky, studded with brilliant stars, and let the beauty of the scenery and the peaceful surroundings relax me.

On the way back we barely spoke, but as soon as the boat was tied up he pulled me into his arms and, without warning, kissed me with such strength that I was almost knocked off my feet. When I got my breath back, I said, 'I don't understand you, Johnny Sheerin. You were so cut off earlier. Now this?'

'Ellie, we have something special between us,' he said, moving closer. 'You know we do, don't you?' he asked, shakily, as though terrified I might say no. As if to prove it, he kissed me again. There was something frightening in the urgency of his kiss. 'I want you to stay in Lisheen, be part of my life.'

Shocked, I looked at him. He was deadly serious. 'This is all too sudden,' I said. 'I can't do that, Johnny.'

'Why not? It isn't as if we're strangers. We've known one another all of our lives.'

'I know that, but we've only just become reacquainted.'

'It was when you left that I realised how much I loved you.' Startled, I looked at him. 'Ellie, not many people become as close to one another as we have over the years. Or maybe I'm wrong. Maybe you don't feel like that about me any more.'

'Of course I feel close to you, Johnny.' Even I couldn't believe the closeness I felt to him at that moment. The unspoken feeling of understanding that had existed before I left Ireland was back.

He was silent for some time. I wondered if his declaration of love had been an embarrassment to him.

'I'm sorry if I sprang this on you, Ellie,' he said. 'But I can't bear the thought of saying goodbye to you again.'

'I have to go back to the States, Johnny.'

'Is that where you see yourself in a few years' time?' he asked. 'Will you come back, or will you stay there?'

'It's hard to tell,' I said truthfully. 'I may have a string of shops over there, or I might be sitting in the back room of Aunt Mabel's shop with all her memorabilia cluttered around me.'

He walked a short distance, then turned back. 'Please don't go, Ellie,' he pleaded. 'How often do you think I can keep losing you?' he asked. This time his kiss was desperate, as though in it he would find the reassurance he was looking for. I was surprised that Johnny, with all his strength, should be the needy one for a change. I'd never considered that possibility before.

I pulled back, tearfully. 'I have to get back, there's a lot of clearing up to do.'

Silently, we returned to the cottage and the dying celebrations.

Twenty-Four

Dressed in a suit, looking well-groomed and handsome, Johnny loaded my suitcase into his trap and off we went, Mam with Matthew in her arms, Lucy, Ed, and Maura all waving their goodbyes. As we drove through Lisheen, I closed my eyes so I wouldn't have to look at the village as we passed it.

The sky was blue, the sea calm. Halfway to Cobh, Johnny turned off into a sidestreet in a town and stopped outside a hotel. 'I thought we should have a meal out before you go off again,' he said.

The meal was delicious, but I had no appetite for it.

'Not hungry?' Johnny asked, as I picked at my food.

'No, I'm just nervous thinking about the journey.'

Resting his knife and fork on his plate he said, 'You don't have to go, Ellie.'

I met his gaze. 'I must go, Johnny. I thought you of all people would understand that.'

'You see America as the solution to all of your problems. You're using it like an insurance policy. You think it'll cover every part of your future. You think it will never let you down,' he said accusingly.

'That's what I have to believe. I figure I can't leave it now. There are things I have to do, commitments I've made to other people. And I can't wait to see Alice again.'

'See, you're talking like a Yank already.' He looked at me closely. 'Ellie, what about the part I could play in your life?'

I shook my head. 'I can't make any promises to you at the moment, Johnny.'

'You'd rather try and manage everything all by yourself than have me?'

'I'm not saying that. I don't know what the future holds. Please Johnny, try to understand.'

He finished his meal half-heartedly.

At the docks in Cobh, I said to him, 'I'll write to you; I'll keep writing, all of the time.'

'Promise me that you will.'

'I promise.' I kissed him goodbye and followed the other passengers to the open door. Pausing for a brief moment on the threshold, I turned to wave to him. He waved back. His sad eyes followed me as I stepped through the door and into the departure area.